At Issue

Are Adoption
Policies Fair?

Other Books in the At Issue Series:

At Issue

Are Adoption Policies Fair?

Amanda Hiber, Book Editor

HV
875.55
A74
2008

GREENHAVEN PRESS
A part of Gale, Cengage Learning

GALE
CENGAGE Learning

Detroit • New York • San Francisco • New Haven, Conn • Waterville, Maine • London

Christine Nasso, *Publisher*
Elizabeth Des Chenes, *Managing Editor*

© 2008 Greenhaven Press, a part of Gale, Cengage Learning.

Gale and Greenhaven Press are registered trademarks used herein under license.

For more information, contact:
Greenhaven Press
27500 Drake Rd.
Farmington Hills, MI 48331-3535
Or you can visit our Internet site at gale.cengage.com

For product information and technology assistance, contact us at

Gale Customer Support, 1-800-877-4253
For permission to use material from this text or product, submit all requests online at www.cengage.com/permissions

Further permissions questions can be emailed to permissionrequest@cengage.com

Articles in Greenhaven Press anthologies are often edited for length to meet page requirements. In addition, original titles of these works are changed to clearly present the main thesis and to explicitly indicate the author's opinion. Every effort is made to ensure that Greenhaven Press accurately reflects the original intent of the authors. Every effort has been made to trace the owners of copyrighted material.

Cover photograph reproduced by permission of © Images.com/Corbis.

LIBRARY OF CONGRESS CATALOGING-IN-PUBLICATION DATA

Are adoption policies fair? / Amanda Hiber, book editor.
   p. cm. -- (At issue)
   Includes bibliographical references and index.
   ISBN-13: 978-0-7377-3910-7 (hardcover)
   ISBN-13: 978-0-7377-3911-4 (pbk.)
   1. Adoption--Government policy--United States--Juvenile literature. I. Hiber, Amanda.
   HV875.55.A74 2008
   362.734--dc22
                                                           2008007484

Printed in the United States of America
1 2 3 4 5 6 7 12 11 10 09 08

Contents

Introduction

Adoption policy has become front-page news in recent years. Along with the continuing debate of birth mothers' rights versus the rights of adoptive parents and adoptees, birth fathers' rights are now being more publicly considered. In 2006 Arizona's legislature attempted to put into effect a policy that would give married couples preference over single adults in adoption, but the bill was defeated. States increasingly are instituting partial bans on adoptions by gays and lesbians, and in 2004 a U.S. Circuit Court of Appeals upheld Florida's outright ban on adoption by gays and lesbians. Finally, the policies of countries, including the United States, with regard to international adoption, have made major headlines, most notably in late 2006 when the Chinese government announced that it would begin barring adoptions to foreigners who are over age fifty, single, obese, or do not meet a number of other standards.

All this talk about adoption might lead the average news consumer to conclude that adoptions have become vastly more common, that the number of adoptions in the United States has simply shot up. In fact, this is not the case. The Evan B. Donaldson Adoption Institute explains: "For a variety of societal and economic reasons, there have been dramatic fluctuations in the annual number of adoptions. For instance, adoptions skyrocketed from a low of 50,000 in 1944 to a high of 175,000 in 1970. In 1992, the last year for which reliable numbers were available, there were almost 127,000 annual adoptions in the U.S." In its 2007 *Adoption Factbook IV*, the National Council for Adoption reports a total of 151,332 adoptions in 2002—still well below the 1970 high.

Within these totals, however, certain types of adoptions have shown a dramatic increase over the past few decades—most demonstrably, international adoptions. In her 2002 testimony before the House Committee on International Relations, Cindy Freidmutter, executive director of the Adoption Institute, said, "Over the last decade, the number of international adoptions by Americans has increased threefold from about 6,500 in 1992 to over 19,000 in 2001." Adoptions by gays and lesbians have also been on the rise. A 2007 study by the nonpartisan Urban Institute found that gay and lesbian parents are now raising approximately 4 percent of all adopted children in the United States.

While the total number of adoptions has not seen a consistent change in one direction or another, studies show that recent decades *have* seen a consistent change in Americans' attitudes toward adoption. A 2002 National Adoption Attitudes Survey by the Adoption Institute revealed: "The proportion of Americans with very favorable opinions about adoption increased to 63% in 2002, from 56% in 1997. The number with very and somewhat favorable opinions rose from 90% to 94%." There has also been an increase in the number of Americans who have considered adoption themselves. This shift in attitudes is clearly correlated with how much contact Americans have with those going through the adoption process, on either end. The same study found that "in 2002, 64% of respondents reported that a family member or close friend had been adopted, had adopted, or had placed a child for adoption, up from 58% in 1997."

This sizable increase indicates that adoption has moved into the mainstream, in terms of Americans' experiences and attitudes. Whereas adoption was once seen as an exceptional situation unique to a specific group of Americans, adoptive families and adoptees have now been integrated into ordinary Americans' communities and daily lives. This relaxing of attitudes can even be seen within the adoption community, as Albert R. Hunt points out in his *Wall Street Journal* article, "Slow But Steady Progress on Adoption": "Contact between birth and adoptive parents, once taboo, is becoming more common now. This kind of transparency is a sign of enormous progress from the old days when adoption's secretive nature made it a stigma."

No longer a secret, adoption is now an issue of interest to wide numbers of Americans—and as a result, so are the policies that dictate who may adopt, and how and where they may adopt. Many of these policies—from open records laws to putative father registries—are discussed in *At Issue: Are Adoption Policies Fair?* As adoption continues to affect more and more Americans, the issues debated here become ever more relevant.

1

Open Adoption Policies Are Fair

Lorraine Dusky

Lorraine Dusky is the author of Birthmark, *a memoir about giving her daughter up for adoption. She is the New York representative to the American Adoption Congress.*

On January 1, 2005 New Hampshire joined six other states in passing a law that grants adoptees access to their birth records. This law provides a momentous opportunity to those who wish to learn the identities of their birth parents. Bills proposing to open birth records have faced strong opposition from those arguing that women who gave up their children for adoption decades ago were promised anonymity and open adoption bills would betray these promises. As one of these women, I was not promised anonymity; rather, I was given no option but anonymity. Many years later, I sought contact with my daughter and paid someone to locate her. I am now happily reunited with her, and I wish other women in my position would be given the same opportunity.

On Monday [January 3, 2005] Janet Allen plans to walk into the Division of Vital Records Administration in Concord, N.H., and ask for a copy of her original birth certificate. It will be the first time she can legally obtain it.

Allen, 51, a state legislator, was adopted as an infant. In New Hampshire, where she was born and adopted, Allen has been denied the right to that singular piece of paper that contains the answer to one of life's most basic questions: Who am I? The change in the law occurs two days from now, New Years Day, 2005. As one of the people who worked for the bill's passage, Allen will be first in line.

"I am no longer a child and am delighted to finally have the same rights as non-adopted adults," she says. "The law now guarantees that no one will ever again have to go before a judge to beg, plead and be humiliated for a piece of paper that belongs to him."

Why does it matter so much to her and thousands of other adopted people in the state? Because her original birth certificate—not the amended one she's had most of her life—contains the names of her birth parents, and thus the key to her identity and origin. With the names, adopted people can search out their natural parents and perhaps obtain not only answers, but also updated medical information as well as the possibility of an ongoing relationship.

With the law's passage, New Hampshire will joined six other states—Alabama, Alaska, Delaware, Kansas, Tennessee and Oregon—that allow individuals adopted as children the right to their original birth certificates.

Some states had open birth records until the 1960s and even into [the] 1980s. But as adoption became more common following the sexual revolution of those times, most of the states left with open records closed them, sweeping aside the rights of adopted children, no matter their age, to investigate their origins.

An Uphill Legislative Battle

The bills to modernize the laws encounter stiff opposition and intense lobbying in state legislatures everywhere from adoption agencies and attorneys, local Catholic charities, the Church of Jesus Christ of Latter-Day Saints, and state chapters of the American Civil Liberties Union.

Against these well-funded organizations, the impassioned pleas of adoptees asking for open records are nearly drowned out, even though they are the ones whose rights should be tantamount.

In numerous states, bills to open the records have either languished in committee or died at the end of a legislative session. The opposition always hinges on the supposed anonymity that the women who gave up their children 30, 40 years ago were promised then, and are said to fervently desire today.

The vast majority of us desperately want to know our children.

I am one of those women, and I was not "promised" anonymity from my daughter. It was forced on me like a pair of manacles. The relinquishment papers gave me no opportunity to confirm or deny whether I might want to know her one day. There were no boxes to check marked either "contact desired" or "no contact." The papers merely stated that I was turning over my daughter to the state. The document promised nothing, not even that she would be adopted.

Our forced anonymity is a by-product of laws that seal the original birth certificate from the adopted person, designed to give adoptive parents the feeling their adopted children are really "theirs." Love was expected to quell curiosity. We birth mothers were supposed to "get on with our lives."

I protested to my social worker because never to know my own child sounded like living death. But I felt I had no choice; I signed the papers.

Few Want Anonymity

I am not alone. The vast majority of us desperately want to know our children. We pray for the knock on the door, the phone call that will begin our healing.

How many of us are there? Probably between 5 million and 6 million, given the best estimate of "stranger" adoptions, those in which the baby is not given to a family member. How many of us seek reunion? There is no accurate way to know. But data from Oregon, which has allowed adoptees access to their original birth certificates since 2000, is as good an indicator as any.

As part of the new law, Oregon gave birth mothers, as well as fathers, a chance to file a "no contact" preference. Near the end of 2004, nearly 8,000 adoptees had requested and received their original birth certificates. Eighty-three birth parents had asked for no contact, just a smidgeon over 1 percent.

In New Hampshire, the group of adoptees and birth parents who fought for open records has sent an e-mail alert that has been bouncing around the Web for the last month, trying to ferret out New Hampshire birth mothers, assuming most will want to update their names and addresses so their children can find them.

Of course, there will be some who ask for no contact.

I am no longer the terrified young thing I was back in 1966.

I try to sympathize with those women who want to hide from their own children. Perhaps they never told their husbands or their other children. Perhaps they have buried the secret so deeply—because it hurts too much to do otherwise—that they can not even imagine dealing with a flesh-and-blood person who asks "why?" Perhaps they are too guilty to face the child, now grown.

Who I Was Then and Who I Am Now

If you knew me when my daughter was born, in 1966 in Rochester, N.Y., you might guess I would be one of them today. The father, a married man with a public life, had to be "pro-

13

tected." For his sake, and yes, mine, I operated in deepest secrecy. A Catholic girl a year out of college, so deep was my shame that I hid my pregnancy from my family in another state.

But times and attitudes change. As far back as 1980, after holding numerous hearings around the country, the then Department of Health, Education and Welfare proposed a Model Adoption Act that would have opened the records.

"There can be no legally protected interest in keeping one's identity secret from one's biological offspring; parents and child are considered co-owners of the information regarding the event of birth," it stated. "The birth parents' interest in reputation is not alone deserving of constitutional protection." But while some provisions of the act became national policy, this did not.

I am no longer the terrified young thing I was back in 1966.

Years ago, I decided I couldn't wait for Congress, or New York's legislature, to act. I paid a searcher $1,200. Within weeks I had my daughter's name and phone number and made that scary phone call to her other mother. Our daughter was still a teen-ager. I met her and her family in a matter of days.

That was more than two decades ago.

At my daughter's wedding, I stood next to her other mother during the ceremony. Yes, I was the one who didn't know a lot of people there, but my brothers and their wives, and some of their kids, were there too. It was a happy event for everyone. It was as it should be.

2

Open Adoption Is Only Fair with the Consent of All Parties

Thomas C. Atwood

Thomas C. Atwood is president and chief executive officer of the National Council for Adoption, an adoption research, education, and advocacy organization.

New Hampshire Senate Bill 335 proposes making all adoptions— past, present, and future—open adoptions, regardless of involved parties' preferences. Open adoptions are frequently represented by the media as having unanimous support, yet in reality many of the people involved in adoptions wish to maintain their anonymity. This bill would make public identifying information about birth parents and adoptees, thereby violating the privacy rights of all involved parties. Furthermore, it would have several negative secondary effects such as weakening the adoptive family and reducing the number of adoptions, thereby increasing the number of abortions and children in foster care. Open adoptions should remain a matter of choice for birth parents and adoptees. Identifying information should only be released with the consent of both adult adoptees and their birth parents.

The right to maintain or waive one's privacy in adoption is essential to the human rights and personal dignity of adopted persons, birthparents, and adoptive parents. Adoption policy and practice should not empower one party to adoption to receive identifying information or unilaterally impose contacts without the consent of another party. Birthparents and adult adopted persons who desire to have contact should be able to do so, when *both* agree. Otherwise, both should be able to control the release of their identifying information and whether and when contacts are to occur.

Search and reunion advocacy is commonplace in the media, but the range of views among birthparents, adopted persons, and adoptive parents regarding confidentiality and openness in adoption are actually as diverse and personal as they can be. The only just way to reconcile these varying views is through mutual consent, not unilateral coercion. Yet SB335 [New Hampshire Senate Bill 335, which allows adult adoptees to obtain their birth certificates and allows birth parents to express their preferences regarding contact with adoptees] would impose a one-size-fits-all, mandatory openness policy on all adoptions, past, present, and future. It would eliminate New Hampshire's current humane policy based on mutual consent and replace it with a policy based on unilateral coercion.

Unfortunately, the loudest voices the legislature and the general public are likely to hear regarding SB335 belong to a small minority who demand the right for adopted persons to identify and contact their birthparents, with or without their consent. It is important to note, however, that the many who prefer privacy cannot discuss their views publicly without sacrificing the very privacy they desire to protect. Birthparents who desire to maintain confidentiality must either remain mute while their rights are being taken away or lose their confidentiality in the very act of defending it. The National Council For Adoption speaks in their defense, and in defense of the institution of adoption and of the children, families, and birthparents it serves.

Harmful Effects

There are several ways that SB335's elimination of confidentiality in adoption would harm adoption, children, families, and birthparents:

- **First, SB335 would violate birthparents' basic human right to privacy.** SB335 would completely eliminate birthparents' right to choose a confidential adoption, both retroactively and prospectively. To open records retroactively without the approval of a birthmother who was promised privacy is a particularly egregious violation of trust and common decency. For the typical birthmother, making an adoption plan for her child is a supremely loving act, committed in the best interests of her child. The state of New Hampshire should honor birthmothers for this act of love, not punish them by stripping them of their basic human right to privacy.

- Under SB335, no future birthmother in New Hampshire would be allowed to choose a private adoption, no matter what the circumstances of pregnancy or birth. Without the right to choose a confidential adoption, the birthmother who felt she must have privacy would have no choice but abortion. As stated by Jeremiah Gutman, director of the American Civil Liberties Union (ACLU) and former chair of the ACLU's Privacy Committee, a woman facing an unplanned pregnancy could maintain her privacy *only* if she had an abortion. Would the state of New Hampshire grant a woman with an unplanned pregnancy a right to private abortion but not to private adoption?

- We ask the House Children and Family Law Committee to recognize that there are any number of legitimate and understandable reasons that birthparents may desire privacy—perhaps, the birthmother does not want to relive the experience of rape or incest that caused the pregnancy; perhaps the birthparent would be psychologically or emotionally unable or unready to handle the stress of renewed contact; perhaps the birthparent does not want to upset his or her spouse, family, and friends with a never shared revelation; or perhaps the birthparent simply believes that the healthiest approach for all parties is not to have an ongoing relationship. Does the state of New Hampshire truly believe that one-size-fits-all, mandatory open records is a superior policy to respecting birthparents' loving discernment and their right to privacy?

Disrupting Lives

- **Second, SB335 would increase the number of unwanted, unilaterally imposed contacts and wreak havoc in people's lives.** Providing adult adopted persons identifying birthparent information without birthparents' knowledge or approval would, obviously, increase the number of unwanted, unilaterally imposed contacts. Thousands of New Hampshire birthparents, around the country and world, would be unaware that their privacy was eliminated by this law. And even if they were aware of it, they would be powerless to prevent unwanted contacts or control the timing of them. SB335's contact preference form does nothing to enable birthparents to control whether and when reunions would occur. Unwanted reunions between adult adopted persons and birthparents are often highly disruptive and unsatisfactory for everyone involved, despite the rosy scenarios sometimes portrayed in the media. Even when adopted persons and birthparents mutually consent to contact, their satisfaction with reunions and ongoing relationships is quite unpredictable.

- **Third, SB335 would undermine the strength of the adoptive family,** by establishing as the legal norm and the cultural expectation that adopted persons and their birthparents will, and should, "reunite" when the child reaches the age of majority. A chief reason adoption has been so successful is because society and law have respected the adoptive family as the child's true and permanent family. But SB335 would promote the view of the adoptive family as not much more than long-term foster care, until the adopted child grows up and can be reunited with her or his "real" family. Such a view is harmful to children and families. Adoptive parenting has provided untold social and familial blessings to children throughout the years. Law and society must continue to respect the adoptive family's status as the adopted person's true and permanent family, in order for those blessings to continue.

Reduced Numbers of Adoptions

- **Fourth, SB335 would reduce the number of adoptions and increase the number of abortions.** "Open-records" advocates' argument that eliminating the option of confidentiality in adoption would have no effect on the number of abortions defies common sense. Obviously, some number of women with unplanned pregnancies, who would otherwise choose adoption, would choose abortion if they could not choose adoption with the assurance of privacy. What that number would be is impossible to tell, but what does it need to be? The loss of human potential from even one abortion that would have been an adoption is unknowable. And the ratio of adoptions to abortions in New Hampshire is already extremely low. In 1996, New Hampshire had only 43 domestic infant adoptions placements for every 1,000 abortions.

- **Fifth, SB335 would reduce the number of adoptions and increase the number of children in foster care.** Eliminating privacy in adoption would mean that women with unplanned, out-of-wedlock births, who would only choose adoption if it was confidential, would have no choice but to single-parent. Social science data clearly reveal that the more single parents there are, the more children languish in foster care, with greatly increased social and economic costs as a result. Additionally, fewer couples would be willing to adopt, because of the promotion of the view of adoption as long-term foster care, and because of heightened fear over birthparents' ability to disrupt the adoptive family. With fewer families willing to adopt, more children would be stuck in foster care for longer periods of time.

No Benefits for Adoptees

- **Sixth, SB335 would perpetuate the myth that adopted persons face debilitating identity problems** that can only be resolved by mandatory open records and reunions with birthparents. The erroneous assumption of mandatory open-records advocates is the false and demeaning notion that in order to be psychologically healthy, all adopted persons must fulfill a deep-seated need to have identifying information about, and contact with, their biological parents. The truth is, however, that the vast majority of persons adopted at a young age accept their adoption readily, and grow up to be successful, happy, stable adults at the same rate as people raised in their biological families. While many adopted persons indicate a curiosity about their biological parents, very few profess anything approaching a need for identifying information or contact. Fewer still would favor having the right to impose themselves on birthparents against their will, and only a small percentage actually search.

- **Seventh, SB335 would add nothing to the adopted person's ability to obtain medical information.** New Hampshire law already allows for adopted persons to obtain birthparent health history without sacrificing confidentiality. Agencies and attorneys alike willingly facilitate this process confidentially. In addition, genetic testing available today makes this issue moot. One can obtain far more information about one's genetic predispositions from such tests than from any medical history of biological parents.

Mutual Consent

Birthparents and adult adopted persons who desire to exchange identifying information and/or have contact with each other should be allowed to do so. New Hampshire's existing Chapter 170-B:19 already provides for that. By allowing birthparents to sign, at the time of relinquishment or consent to adoption, a release authorizing the adult adopted person to obtain birthparent identifying information, and also allowing the birthparent the right to revoke or amend the permission at any time, New Hampshire is already facilitating mutually desired contact, while allowing birthparents to safeguard their privacy, if they so choose. Though one may sympathize with the adopted person who desires to know his or her birthparents personally, mutual consent is the only fair standard for the sharing of identifying information and for contacts between adopted persons and their birthparents.

Opponents of the principle of mutual consent often attempt to justify their opposition by stating that the low frequency of reunions is evidence of the policy's ineffectiveness. The more likely explanation is that those who have not registered their interest in contact simply have chosen not to share identifying information or have contact. People who so choose should be allowed to keep their privacy. Existing law that allows birthparents to authorize, as part of the adoption approval process, release of their identifying information to the adult adopted child, has the effect of making birthparents aware of the option to forgo privacy.

No other counseling relationship between client and professional service provider is subject to state violation of client privacy. If the state may remove a professionally guaranteed right to confidentiality in adoption, what is to prevent the state from attempting to remove that right in relationships with doctors, lawyers, clergy, and others, as well? Eliminating privacy in adoption resulted in the elimination of adoption as a viable social institution in Great Britain. It would be tragic and devastating to the interests of children to see that outcome in New Hampshire. But the same result could well occur here if SB335 is enacted, to the detriment of children, birthparents, and families.

3

Photolists of Children Awaiting Adoption Raise Ethical Concerns

Sarah Gerstenzang and Madelyn Freundlich

Sarah Gerstenzang is the assistant project director of the Collaboration to AdoptUsKids at the Adoption Exchange Assocation. She is a former senior policy analyst at Children's Rights, Inc. Madelyn Freundlich is policy director for Children's Rights, Inc., and was formerly executive director of the Evan B. Donaldson Adoption Institute.

The large number of children in foster care who are awaiting adoptive families requires that child welfare agencies try different strategies to recruit such families. One of these strategies is online photolistings, which include photographs and short descriptions, of children awaiting adoption. Unlike past approaches, Internet listings can reach millions of people and interest families who may never have actively sought out adoption. But as agencies use this method, they must be aware of some ethical issues raised by photolisting. Warning signs of inappropriate use of photolistings include detailed information about a child's past traumas, language that resembles product marketing, and descriptions that perpetuate stereotypes. Child welfare professionals need to develop guidelines that determine how much information should be included, and what kind of information is appropriate, in online descriptions. These guidelines must take into account both ethical and legal privacy limitations. While

Sarah Gerstenzang and Madelyn Freundlich, "Should We Photolist Waiting Children?" *Children's Voice*, November-December 2003. Copyright © Child Welfare League of America. All rights reserved. Reproduced by permission.

photolisting has proven to be an effective tool in the placement of children with adoptive families, it must be used with caution and foresight.

As of September 2000, 75,000 children in foster care were free for adoption—a number that continues to grow each year, placing greater demands on child welfare systems to find adoptive families. State and local agencies have used different strategies to recruit adoptive families—including photolistings, which allow potential adoptive parents to view pictures and read short descriptions of available children.

Since 1994, photolistings have been posted on the Internet, either on individual states' websites or the federally funded website known since 2002 as AdoptUsKids. This national website currently lists 3,000 children in foster care who are available for adoption.

Before the Internet, families interested in adopting children from foster care typically visited child welfare agencies and reviewed photographs and biographies of children who were available for adoption in their own states. Later, agencies partnered with local newspapers and television stations to develop feature articles and television spots such as "Wednesday's Child" to alert the public to the needs of waiting children.

Unlike these earlier approaches, however, the Internet has the capacity to reach millions of people and interest families who may never have been made aware of children in foster care who needed adoptive families. Among its benefits, the Internet offers ready access to information in a cost-efficient manner, and privacy for families who may be in the early stages of considering adoption but not be ready to contact a social service agency.

As child welfare systems have recognized the benefits of this new means of recruiting families for waiting children, practitioners have confronted some ethical issues, particularly regarding the type of information shared about children in the very public venue of the Internet.

Red Flags

In a random downloading of Internet postings, samples of actual photolistings illustrate the types of information posted about children and raise several ethical issues to consider when the Internet is used as a recruiting tool for adoptive families:

Frequent use of clinical terms to describe children and their behavior or status.

> *[Isabelle] experienced a chaotic life and as a result has been diagnosed with and receives medication and therapy for attention deficit/hyperactivity disorder (ADHD), oppositional defiant disorder, and post-traumatic stress disorder.*

These diagnostic terms aren't likely to be clear to the average reader and lack any context that helps the reader understand how these conditions affect the child.

Highly detailed descriptions of behavior problems, and interpretative comments about the child's behaviors.

> *A very quiet Daquan [age 5] who remains that way for an extended period of time is an indication that he is upset. He might sulk for a long time before he brightens up again.*

Such descriptions, which may describe typical behaviors for children of the age of the featured child, nevertheless seem to suggest a more serious problem.

Highlighting physical and personality aspects that convey [someone] is a "good" child . . . suggests the child is a commodity to be marketed.

References to the child's suspected history, and details about actual past traumas.

> *David entered care as a result of neglect and has experienced many moves in his short life. He is diagnosed with global developmental delays, and it is suspected that he was drug exposed in utero.*

25

Even when described as "suspected," the reference to prenatal drug exposure raises questions about the child's physical and developmental status when, in reality, there is no certainty his history includes this situation.

Highly positive language that sounds like product marketing.

[Harold] is a clean-cut child with good manners, good personal hygiene, and an appreciation for what is done for him.

By highlighting physical and personality aspects that convey he is a "good" child, such language suggests the child is a commodity to be marketed.

Descriptions that reinforce stereotypes.

Michael [a 10-year-old African American boy] has no physical impairments, and his gross muscle [sic] are well developed.

Observations about the muscle development and athletic prowess of African American children appear in many descriptions.

Overly prescriptive comments on necessary parenting styles.

Shirley's foster family says she needs a lot of structure in her life or things can quickly get out of hand. Shirley will need a family that has the patience to keep after her to finish tasks such as homework and household chores. She will need consistency, clearly set guidelines with consequences, and lots of structure.

These types of descriptions, coming in the first introduction to a child, assume the child's response to a foster family will carry forward into her relationship with an adoptive family.

Effects on Children

Equally troubling is how such descriptions in a public venue might affect the featured children. Many people object to photolistings as distasteful "marketing" of children. Most parents would not permit their own child to appear with such detailed personal information in a public forum, and they don't find it appropriate to feature other children this way.

On the other hand, considering the growing number of children in foster care, the ongoing desperate need for thousands of adoptive families, and continued limited funding for recruitment, using every opportunity to expand the pool of adoptive families is imperative. The question is how to make Internet technology work for children in an ethical manner. Recent experiences in Canada provide some insight.

Alberta's privacy commissioner ordered that details about the children's medical and psychiatric problems . . . be removed from their profiles.

More than 4,700 children in foster care in Alberta were freed for adoption in 2002, but only 116—less than 3%—were adopted. In an attempt to increase the number of adoptions, Alberta Children's Services launched a website featuring waiting children in February 2003. The website, which included photographs, written profiles, and video clips of the children, sought families only within Alberta unless exceptional circumstances dictated otherwise.

The website generated tremendous controversy. Aside from a general anxiety about whether the listings would attract sexual predators, several concrete practice concerns arose. Featured children were teased at school by classmates who had read some of their medical and social histories online, and some children weren't aware that families were being sought to adopt them.

Alberta's privacy commissioner ordered that details about the children's medical and psychiatric problems and their histories of abuse be removed from their profiles. The Ministry of Children's Services delayed featuring additional children until the site was evaluated after a three-month trial.

Despite these problems, less than two weeks after the website's launch, the agency removed 13 of the 93 children originally featured because 40 potential adoptive families had expressed interest in adopting a featured child. By May, three months into the first year of operation, 48 children had been matched with potential adoptive families, including 12 who weren't actually listed on the website.

Ethical Guidelines

The goal of photolisting is straightforward: to find families for children. To achieve this goal, photolistings have several objectives:

- alert families to waiting children;

- provide potential adoptive families with individualized descriptions of featured children;

- provide information to interested families on steps to take to learn more about the child and the adoption process; and

- interest families in adopting other children from foster care if a featured child is no longer available for adoption or the family is not a good fit for the child.

Where does information posted on the Internet fit within the continuum of information sharing in the adoption process? Professionals generally agree that photolistings on the Internet serve as a recruiting tool and should include some information about the child. The question is, how much information?

Disclosing information to adoptive parents about children's backgrounds and status is important from an ethical perspective, but the very public venue of the Internet raises questions about the extent to which personal information on children should be shared in that forum. "Too much information too soon" seems to have become all too frequent, raising the need to closely examine what is [the] best practice.

In developing guidelines for providing information on the Internet about children in foster care, we need to address three issues:

What Information Should Be Included?

Professionals have access to both objective and subjective information for children featured in photolistings. Objective information includes a child's appearance, or an actual photograph, and the child's age or birth date, racial and ethnic background, and any diagnosed medical conditions. Objective information in a photolisting usually doesn't raise ethical concerns.

Subjective information, however—such as a child's strengths, problems, challenges, disabilities, or needs regarding an adoptive family—is often far more problematic. Any subjective information that may be posted should be carefully assessed for its usefulness and appropriateness. Is the information actually "known," being reasonably guessed at, or very speculative? Even if it is "actually known," the information should be examined critically to determine whether it is complete, up-to-date, and from a reliable source.

How a child's photolisting is developed is also critical . . . because information can be easily misconstrued.

This issue is important in constructing initial Internet postings and in ensuring the accuracy of postings that remain on the Internet for a length of time. Photolistings are usually updated infrequently—often just yearly. Agencies using photolistings should take care to ensure information remains fresh and accurate.

Consider the following description of a 6-year-old:

> John began taking classes under the Early Childhood Intervention program and will need to continue these classes until he enters kindergarten.

Although the listing agency updated the child's age, it failed to update information written before he entered kindergarten. Thus, the listing not only misstates his current school status, it suggests the issues for which he received early intervention services persist, which may or may not be accurate.

How a child's photolisting is developed is also critical. Has the writer of the child's description ever met the child? How was the information collected? Has someone who knows the child, such as a foster parent, reviewed the information for accuracy? Did the child help write a descriptive paragraph? These issues are critical because information can be easily misconstrued.

Case in point: Sarah Gerstenzang, a foster parent and one of the authors of this article, adopted a child in her care in September 2002. The medical summary prepared from the child's case record in preparation for adoption stated the child was "examined on January 5, 2002 . . . and was found to have the following conditions. . . ." Two of the conditions listed were "prenatal exposure to illicit substances" and "mild to moderate developmental delays."

As the girl's foster parent, Sarah knew the January exam was just a check-up and was unremarkable; that there was no evidence the child had ever been exposed to illicit substances, although there was some family history; and that the referenced developmental delays were noted in an exam in 2000 when the child was 4 months old. At age 2, the little girl was thriving, but the medical summary was so intimidating and inaccurate that Sarah's lawyer advised the child be classified as "special needs."

The presentation of the information is equally important, given the goal of attracting families. To ensure against misspellings, typos, or missed or repeated words, child profiles should be proofread before posting.

Privacy Concerns

Limits on sharing information based on privacy may be either ethical or legal. Ethically, officials must consider the child's age, her understanding of the photolisting process, and her grasp of the possible implications of being photolisted. Birth-family, friends, and community members may be able to access the child's personal information. Officials must acknowledge the child's understanding of the process and such possibilities as school friends seeing her on the Internet and reading about her background.

Decisions about posting specific health and mental health information should be based on several considerations—the seriousness of the condition; how recent the occurrence; the relationship, if any, between the problem and the child's current environment; and how the condition would affect the child and the prospective family.

Listings that include diagnostic labels without any context for such information is of particular concern. Pediatrician Lisa Albers, with the Developmental Medicine Center and Adoption Program at Children's Hospital in Boston, emphasizes that childhood emotional and behavioral disorders are diagnosed through observations and reports of behaviors and tend to be less definitive than a medical diagnosis based on an x-ray or blood test:

> Sometimes the diagnosis is well described by an alphabet soup (RAD, PTSD, ODD, ADHD, etc.), but in my experience, those letters only shed light on one facet of any given child. In addition, children with any one of these diagnoses may present very differently from another child with the exact same diagnosis or diagnoses.

Legal constraints also limit publicly sharing certain information. Privacy laws in most states prohibit sharing information about adult members of the birthfamily. Some states require a court order to photolist a child. By law, a child's HIV [human immunodeficiency virus] status may not be disclosed publicly. Finally, privacy regulations under the Health Insurance Portability and Accountability Act (HIPAA) could significantly limit the types of information posted in photolistings. HIPAA sets rigorous standards to protect individuals' health information from disclosure. States thus far have varied in their interpretation of how or whether this law applies to child welfare issues.

Can Practice Support Appropriate Information Sharing?

Because the Internet makes possible the transmission of information to millions of people, it raises unique practice issues. Internet photolistings allow families who may be in the early stages of considering adoption to view children anonymously, bring significantly greater attention to the needs of waiting children, and alert families to waiting children in other states.

We need to understand much more about the effectiveness of Internet photolistings as a recruitment tool.

Child welfare's capacity to meet the response that Internet photolistings can generate, however, remains undeveloped. In many communities, social workers are overwhelmed with the number of inquiries generated by newer, more effective transmissions of information. In some communities, photolistings provide extensive negative information about children to dissuade families whom officials may view as inappropriate resources from contacting the agency. If they are to use the Internet to recruit families, child welfare agencies must be able to respond to inquiries, provide information, and engage families in the adoption process.

Strengthening Photolistings

Photolisting websites can be strengthened to more effectively alert families to the needs of waiting children and educate them about adopting. These websites should contain information—or links to sites with accurate information—that helps potential adoptive families understand such complexities as

- the definition of the term special needs—from a physical or mental health disability to the child being placed for adoption as a member of a sibling group—and how states define special needs differently;

- general qualifications to adopt, such as marital status, age, and other requirements;

- the availability of adoption subsidies and tax credits for special needs adoption;

- a basic explanation of foster care, termination of parental rights, and the adoption process;

- interstate adoptions, transracial adoptions, and adopting older children; and

- perhaps most importantly, information about the number of families who adopt successfully each year from the foster care system, including profiles of families who have done so and links to foster and adoptive support groups nationwide.

We need to understand much more about the effectiveness of Internet photolistings as a recruitment tool, especially compared with other recruitment methods. Do users of photolisting websites obtain the information they need? How does the quality or uniqueness of children's biographies influence adoptive families' decisionmaking? How do caseworkers' responses to calls resulting from photolistings affect families' decisions to go forward?

4

Intraracial Adoptions Should Be Prioritized over Transracial Adoptions

North America Council on Adoptable Children (NACAC)

North American Council on Adoptable Children (NACAC) is an advocacy organization that promotes and supports permanent families for children in the United States and Canada. NACAC was founded in 1974 by adoptive parents.

Ethnic and racial minority children are represented to a disproportionate extent in the U.S. and Canadian child welfare systems. This must be remedied, by both alleviating discrimination that may be a contributing factor, and by actively supporting birth parents in such communities. When children are being placed in permanent homes, families that share the child's ethnic or racial background should be prioritized because these families will be better able to prepare these children for a racist society. Beyond eradicating any discriminatory practices toward families of color, such families should be actively recruited as potential foster and adoptive parents. When children cannot be placed with families that share their backgrounds, their adoptive families must be educated and encouraged to raise these children with an awareness and appreciation of their cultural identities.

It has long been recognized that children of racial and ethnic minority populations are disproportionately represented in the child welfare system in the United States and Canada.

North America Council on Adoptable Children (NACAC), "Race and Ethnicity in Child Welfare," *Race and Ethnicity in Child Welfare*, August 3, 2005. Reproduced by permission.

What is less clear are the causes of this disproportionality. NACAC [North American Council on Adoptable Children] believes that it is the responsibility of all professionals in the child welfare system to scrutinize their practices to better understand how they may contribute to this disproportionality. NACAC acknowledges that profiling of minority communities often leads to differential reporting of children of color to the child welfare system. Mandatory training is needed for workers on reporting as well as to gain knowledge and understanding about diverse cultures. Moreover, emphasis must be placed on getting services, funding, as well as parent advocates and peer mentors for birth parents whose children are at risk of removal or who are in the system. African American, Native American, and Aboriginal children are not only disproportionately represented in the foster care system, but enter earlier and remain longer than other children. We must take action to remedy inappropriate representation of minority children within the child welfare system.

Children are denied permanent families because people of color face systemic and individual discrimination in the child welfare system. Research shows and NACAC believes that race matters and impacts policy and practice decision making in child welfare. We do not live in a color blind society. The placement of children with a family of like ethnic or racial background is preferable because these families have historically demonstrated the ability to equip children with skills and strengths to combat the ill effects of racism.

NACAC believes that every child should be placed with a family who recognizes preservation of the child's ethnic and cultural heritage as an inherent right. Therefore, education regarding ethnic and cultural heritage must be a local and federal priority. We encourage agencies and parent groups to offer training and support to foster and adoptive families. This will ensure that children have ongoing opportunities to develop an understanding and appreciation of their racial and cultural identity.

Fight Discrimination and Actively Recruit Parents of Every Race

NACAC recognizes that the MEPA [Multiethnic Placement Act of 1994] and IEPA [Interethnic Placement Act of 1996, which amended MEPA] require that public and private agencies not delay or deny the placement of any child for adoption or into foster care on the basis of race, color, or national origin of the child or adoptive or foster parent. NACAC also recognizes that MEPA and IEPA require public and private agencies not to delay or deny to any person the opportunity to become an adoptive or foster parent on the basis of race, color, or national origin of the prospective parent or child.

Recruitment efforts have been documented which successfully demonstrate that minority families exist for minority children.

NACAC believes that child welfare agencies should work to eliminate racial and ethnic discrimination and bias in adoption recruitment, selection, and placement procedures. Active and creative efforts are needed to recruit parents of every race and culture for children needing foster and adoptive parents. NACAC urges public and private agencies to provide for diligent and continuous recruitment of potential foster, adoptive, guardianship, and kinship families who reflect the ethnic and racial diversity of children in the community for whom permanent homes are needed. These recruitment efforts should be documented, which will include measurable outcomes including increased numbers of permanent families of color.

Specialized minority recruitment efforts have been documented which successfully demonstrate that minority families exist for minority children, and which facilitate minority placement. NACAC encourages agencies to hire minority staff, provide specialized counseling, utilize parent support groups, assist with obtaining subsidies, provide information and community resources, and implement public awareness and recruitment campaigns. NACAC is committed to the creative expansion of such methods, which include but are not limited to: utilization of minority adoptive families as recruitment specialists, specialized minority counseling and referral services, mobile community service units, and adoption fairs.

Encourage Diversity

NACAC strongly urges states to comply with, and the federal government to enforce, the Multi-ethnic Placement Act provision that requires recruitment in communities that reflect the racial and ethnic background of children in care.

NACAC believes that community-based (i.e., churches, advocacy groups, and other organizations reflective of populations of color) minority and specialty foster care and adoption agencies offer excellent opportunities for recruiting families who reflect the racial and ethnic background of children in care. States and counties should partner with existing agencies and help develop additional programs to support the recruitment of families of color.

Full appreciation and consideration should be given to the child's need for close . . . interaction with his/her culture of origin.

NACAC urges agencies to undertake adequate training for adoption workers to enhance their knowledge of identity, cultural, and ethnic issues in working with African American, Latino, Aboriginal, and Native American children and families. In addition, NACAC believes that adoption organizations and agencies should actively recruit African American, Latino, Aboriginal, and Native American social workers. Foster care and adoption agency staff should receive training to: a) partner with communities of color to assess strengths of potential foster and adoptive families; b) identify barriers which prevent families from successfully adopting; and c) better understand MEPA guidelines for diligent recruitment.

Children's opinions should be taken into consideration in deciding whether transracial placements are in their best interest. If a transracial placement occurs, agencies should be required to provide additional support to preserve children's racial and cultural connections.

Families who do adopt children of ethnic backgrounds different from their own must recognize and understand that the ethnic and cultural heritage of the child is an essential right. The agency should help the family explore the realities of race and racism using resources which include multi-ethnic families and the minority community. It is important for families to consider seeking services and personal contacts in the community that will support the child's ethnicity. NACAC also urges agencies to aid in the development of post-adoption support services for transracial families.

Develop Children's Cultural Identities

When transracial or multi-ethnic placements are made, full appreciation and consideration should be given to the child's need for close identification and interaction with his/her culture of origin. Appropriate family assessment tools should be used when considering all adoptive placements.

Families who adopt transracially should have access to ongoing support services to ensure that children of color have an opportunity to develop a complete understanding of their racial and cultural identity.

5

Transracial Adoptions Should Not Be Discouraged

Katharine Quarmby

Katharine Quarmby is the former home affairs correspondent for The Economist *and a contributing writer to the* Guardian *and* Prospect *magazine. She has authored the children's book,* Fussy Freya, *and* A Question of Blood, *a memoir about her experience as an adoptee.*

A debate over transracial adoption has raged since the 1960s. Some say that transracial adoption is akin to cultural genocide, while others say that a child should be placed with a loving family, no matter their race or ethnicity. I was adopted transracially in the late 1960s by parents who had no preference about their child's race, despite the reluctance of adoption officials. While I definitely faced problems as a half-Persian child in a white family and city, the benefits of being raised by a loving family far outweighed the negative impact of our different races. After a few decades in which transracial adoptions were rare, they became more accepted and common in the 1990s. Yet there are still instances where children wait for a permanent home while authorities search for a same-race family. Although there are advantages to the children in placing them with families who share their backgrounds, the first priority in placement decisions should be matching children with caring, accepting parents.

Some black activists have dubbed it "stealing children" and "cultural genocide". Some adopted adults even call it "transracial abduction". Others reply that it betrays children, abandoning them to a life in short-term foster placements while social workers search for the "perfect match". The controversy over transracial adoption has raged for 30 years, and it is not over yet.

I have a personal interest: I was adopted transracially. In the 1960s, black or mixed-race children were not considered suitable for adoption. I was one of the few mixed-race (in my case half white, half Persian) children who bucked the trend. At the end of yet another session at yet another adoption agency, my father said casually: "We don't mind what colour the baby is." The adoption officer beamed. Perhaps, after all, there was a baby available—me. As I learned from my adoption documents years later, the officer remained concerned that I might "darken too much over the summer months", but luckily that summer was not particularly sunny and she felt able to conclude that "you could hardly call her coloured if you did not know". Freed for adoption with the flourish of a pen, at the age of four months I had a permanent new family—unlike the many other mixed-race or black children of my generation who ended up in poor-quality residential care.

But I stood out in a family of tall, fair boys and, worse, felt isolated in an almost totally white school in Norfolk [England]. I was bullied, punished for being different. I paid a price for growing up as a mixed-race child in an overwhelmingly white county. Research shows that adopted children often outperform non-adopted children educationally. Certainly a motivating factor for me in my studies was the desire to leave Norfolk, and one of the best days of my life was the day I learned I had a place at university and could escape.

The Good Outweighed the Bad

I was raised when the notion of "clean-break" adoption was fashionable. Consequently, I grew up with no knowledge of my Iranian heritage, and I have no friends from Iran and no contact with that country. My birth father—who was serving in the Royal Persian Navy—had wanted to marry my English mother and take us back to Iran, but she wanted to go to university. So I never experienced a Persian childhood. Because that part of my identity is not rooted in any kind of reality, I constantly feel tugged by thoughts about the country and the birth father I never knew. This is called genealogical bewilderment; I feel a part of me has been lost, and I am a stranger to a culture which should have been my own.

I believe that it is more important to experience a loving childhood and belong somewhere than to have a same-race family.

Yet it could have been so much worse. Once my birth mother had refused the offer of marriage and decided to relinquish me, the choices narrowed down to two: adoption or a childhood in the care system. And given that there were not many Iranian families looking to adopt in Leeds [England] in the late 1960s, adoption meant going to a family of a different race. As it happens, my adoptive mother is half Serbian and partly English and Spanish. She arrived as a refugee from Yugoslavia after the war, and her earliest memory of England is of standing in a playground not understanding what was being said. Her experience of the bewilderment of a child who has lost a culture was surely more valuable to me than the colour of her skin (although the adoption agency noted approvingly that she was "on the dark side herself").

Put Children First

No one denies that time in care increases the potential for problems in later life. Ultimately, I believe that it is more important to experience a loving childhood and belong somewhere than to have a same-race family. So I worry when I hear opponents of transracial adoption placing too much emphasis on finding the perfect match. There have long been powerful voices making this case. The Association of Black Social Workers (ABSW) claimed in the 1980s that "transracial placements are a way of perpetuating racist ideology". Their slogan, that "love is not enough", still looms over the argument. They pointed out that white parents did not know how to care for black children's skin or hair, that black children could not walk down the street with their white relatives without having to give an explanation.

ABSW won the argument and transracial adoption became rare, but there remained an acute shortage of same-race adopters and, as a result, children from ethnic minorities still waited longer in care than white children. Then, in the 1990s, research in the US and UK [United Kingdom] concluded that children placed transracially fared as well as those placed in families of the same race. The incoming Labour government was convinced, and in 1998 issued a circular to local authorities, stating: "It is unacceptable for a child to be denied loving adoptive parents solely on the grounds that the child and adopter do not share the same racial and cultural backgrounds." The Home Office minister Paul Boateng said: "We mustn't let dogma get in the way. We have to put children first."

Current Policy and Practice

Seven years on, I wondered whether the policy was being implemented. Most local authorities with which I spoke— among them Manchester, Kent, Liverpool, Lambeth, Westminster, and Hammersmith and Fulham—do place transracially now, particularly where a child is of dual or mixed heritage. Indeed, they point out that it is practically impossible to find a perfect match for all their children, as so many have three or four ethnic backgrounds. Intriguingly, Hammersmith and Fulham and neighbouring Westminster are now fostering transracially—but it is black carers who are looking after white children.

Meryl Sturdy, assistant team manager for Westminster's family placement service, says: "We recognised the impact of drift on children while we were waiting for an ideal ethnic match. Transracial fostering works because of the attitude of the carer. They look beyond skin colour to see a child with needs. We are blowing the concept of same-race placement out of the water."

It is sensible to place children with families of the same race where possible. The question is what to do when this is not possible, and how long the search for the perfect match should go on. Research on attachment theory demonstrates that it is vital that babies be placed in permanent families as quickly as possible; and so I would argue that in principle it is better for a child to go to a good family, even if the family's race or culture is different, than to miss out in the name of that holy grail, the perfect match.

Do Not Make Children Wait

However, there are still many who resist on ideological grounds. I came across an Indian couple who had wanted to adopt a "dual-heritage" child, but found the local authority reluctant—it wanted the child's "white side" to be given priority. And so, the child stayed in foster care for nearly two years. Professor June Thoburn, one of the UK's leading academic experts on adoption, is scathing: "That is crazy—there shouldn't be a delay of this sort." Eventually, the local authority relented and now the boy is happily settled with his new family.

I lost a Persian childhood. . . . But I had love, music, education and stability.

Increasingly, religion is becoming a factor alongside race. When a Sunni Muslim baby was denied a home with a Shia Muslim family, remaining in care for months as a result, even one of the most passionate advocates of same-race placements was horrified, saying that "it felt like policy was being taken to an extreme. There should be time limits on faith matches, especially with a baby." The Department for Education and Skills is so concerned about religion becoming a delaying factor that it has asked Bristol University to investigate. In my case, my mother thinks that my birth father may have been an Armenian Christian who later lived in a secular Iranian family that may casually have observed the Muslim faith. How long would I wait in care these days for the perfect half white, half Iranian, Armenian-Christian/Muslim match?

I lost a Persian childhood: the taste of Persian apricots; the sight of the mountains that ring Tehran [Iran]; the sound of Persian poetry. But I had love, music, education and stability. I gained other childhood memories that shaped my identity: canoeing off the Norfolk coast, the music of Paul Robeson and [Johann Sebastian] Bach in our house, the sight of a barn owl as I walked over Waveney water-meadows. My narrative was fractured by adoption, but I have a voice I would not have had without true, consistent love as a child. I believe transracial and transcultural adoption can work. In the end, love is enough.

6

Gays and Lesbians Should Be Allowed to Adopt

American Civil Liberties Union (ACLU)

The American Civil Liberties Union (ACLU) is a nonprofit, nonpartisan organization founded in 1920. It is dedicated to preserving Americans' rights to equal protection, due process, privacy, and those rights guaranteed by the First Amendment.

Major child welfare organizations have denounced claims that gays and lesbians should be restricted from adopting children, based in part on social scientific evidence that shows that this group is no less fit for parenting than heterosexuals. In addition, child welfare experts have agreed since the 1970s that the best means for placing a child in a home is on a case-by-case basis, rather than ruling out entire groups of people. Such exclusions only result in reducing the number of loving homes for the many children in need of them. Instead of preventing gays and lesbians from adopting, adoption agencies should continue to screen potential parents rigorously and make placement decisions based on the best interest of each particular child.

All of the major children's health and welfare organizations, whose only agenda is to serve the best interest of children, have issued statements opposing restrictions on adopting and fostering by lesbians and gay men. Those policy statements were informed in part by the social science research on lesbian and gay parents and their children, which firmly establishes that there is no child welfare basis for such restrictions because being raised by lesbians or gay men poses no disadvantage to children. But they were also informed by well-established child welfare policy that rejects categorical exclusions of groups of people as contrary to the best interests of children in the child welfare system.

Child welfare experts agree that child placement decisions should be based on children's specific needs and prospective parents' ability to meet those needs. Child welfare professionals understand that every child is unique and has individual needs. Children have diverse personalities, family experiences and physical and emotional needs that all need to be taken into account when making a placement. Similarly, adults seeking to adopt and foster are not all alike. They are diverse individuals who have different skills, qualities, and family environments to offer a child.

Adoption and foster placement is a matching process. Caseworkers seek to find the family that is the best match for each child. For example, one child may fare better with adoptive parents who have other children; another may be better off as an only child. A child may have medical problems and would benefit from being placed with someone who has medical expertise. Some children might do well with a couple; others might be better off with a single parent (e.g., children who have experienced sexual abuse or who need focused attention). In other words, there is no one-size-fits-all when it comes to children. The bigger and more diverse the pool of prospective adoptive and foster parents, the greater the likelihood that placement professionals will be able to make good matches. Categorical exclusions, which throw away individuals who could meet the needs of children, seriously undermine this goal.

Placing a Child

The rejection of blanket exclusions in favor of the principle that placement decisions should be made on a case-by-case basis is well-established in the child welfare field. Indeed, it is reflected in the Child Welfare League of America's Standards of Excellence for Adoption Services [CWLA Standards]:

> When the agency providing adoption services is responsible for selecting the adoptive family, it should base its selection of a family for a particular child on a careful review of the information collected in the child assessment and on a determination of which of the approved and prepared adoptive families could most likely meet the child's needs.

> Applicants should be assessed on the basis of their abilities to successfully parent a child needing family membership and not on their race, ethnicity or culture, income, age, marital status, religion, appearance, differing life style, or sexual orientation.

> Applicants should be accepted on the basis of an individual assessment of their capacity to understand and meet the needs of a particular available child at the point of the adoption and in the future.

Categorical exclusions have become aberrations in child welfare law around the country.

The CWLA Standards are widely accepted as the foundation for sound child welfare practice in the United States. They are a source relied upon by the group's 900 member agencies, which include the state child welfare department in almost every state. The Standards are formulated "based on current knowledge, the developmental needs of children, and tested ways of meeting these needs most effectively." State child welfare departments are significantly involved in the development of the Standards.

Groups No Longer Excluded

Case-by-case evaluation is such a central principle of child welfare practice that categorical exclusions have become aberrations in child welfare law around the country, the only exceptions being for those who have demonstrated conduct that is dangerous to children, such as those convicted of violent crimes or drug offenses. This was not always the case. Until the 1970s, generally only middle-class, white, married, infertile couples in their late twenties to early forties, who were free of any significant disability were considered suitable to adopt. Many agencies excluded applicants who did not meet this ideal such as older couples, low-income families, disabled people, and single adults. But by the 1970s, adoption policy and practice moved away from such exclusions as the field recognized that they were arbitrary and that many individuals who were rejected were valuable parenting resources. It is now the consensus in the child welfare field that case-by-case evaluation is the best practice.

The child welfare professionals agree that the way to ensure healthy, positive placements is to do what every state child welfare agency currently does: subject *every* applicant to a rigorous evaluation process. There are good and bad parents in every group; thus, every applicant must be seriously scrutinized. Whether gay or straight, no one is approved to adopt or foster a child unless he or she clears a child abuse and criminal records check, a reference check, an evaluation of physical and mental health, and a detailed home study that examines the applicant's maturity, family stability, and capacity to parent. Applicants will not be approved unless they are deemed able to protect and nurture and provide a safe, loving family for a child. And no adoption or foster care placement is made unless a caseworker first determines that the placement is the best match available for a particular child. . . .

Depriving Children of Good Parents

Blanket exclusions of lesbians and gay men from adopting or fostering—like any other blanket exclusions—deny children access to available safe, stable, and loving families. For some children, such exclusions mean that they cannot be placed with the family that is best suited to meet their needs. Categorical exclusions tie the hands of caseworkers and prohibit them from making what they deem to be the best placements for some children. For example, a caseworker could not place a child with a gay nurse who is willing to adopt a child with severe medical needs even if there are no other available prospective adoptive parents with the skills necessary to take care of that child. Similarly, a blanket rule would prevent a caseworker from placing a child with a lesbian aunt with whom the child has a close relationship. Instead, that child would have to be placed with strangers, even though the child welfare profession agrees that, wherever possible, children should be placed with relatives.

Blanket exclusions do not just deprive children of the best possible placement. By reducing the number of potential adoptive and foster parents, categorical exclusions of lesbians and gay men condemn many children to a childhood with no family at all. Most states in this country have a critical shortage of adoptive and foster parents. Across the country, more than 118,000 children are waiting to be adopted. Many wait for years in foster care or institutions; some wait out their entire childhoods, never having a family of their own. . . . Many people are not aware of this problem because we often hear about couples who spend years waiting to adopt a baby. But most of the children in the child welfare system in this country are not healthy infants. They are older children and teens, children with serious psychological and behavioral problems, children with challenging medical needs, and groups of siblings who need to be placed together. It is difficult to find families willing to take care of these children.

What This Means

The child welfare agencies go to great lengths to recruit adoptive and foster parents for these children, even posting photos and profiles of waiting children on the Internet. They provide financial subsidies to people who adopt children who are in state care so that the expense of caring for a child is not a barrier to low-income people adopting. Yet thousands of children are still left waiting for families.

The shortage of foster families means that some children get placed far away from their biological families, communities and schools; some get placed in overcrowded foster homes; and some get no foster family at all and instead are placed in institutional settings.

For children waiting to be adopted, the shortage of adoptive families means that some will remain in foster care for years, where they often move around among temporary placements. Some will have to be separated from their siblings in order to be adopted. Some will be placed with families that are not well-suited to meet their needs. And some will never be adopted, and instead "age out" of the system without ever getting to have a family of their own.

Excluding gay people . . . does nothing whatsoever to protect children or promote good placements.

You do not have to be a child welfare expert to understand how scarring it is for a child to grow up without the love and security of a parent. And the scientific research confirms the importance to children's development of forming a parent-child relationship and having a secure family life. Thus, children who are adopted are much less likely than children who spend much of their childhoods in foster care or residential institutions to be maladjusted.

The Long-Term Effects

Young people who age out of foster care without ever becoming part of a family are the most seriously affected. These young people are significantly more likely than their peers to drop out of school, be unemployed, end up homeless and get involved in criminal conduct. According to the federal government, approximately 20,000 young people between the ages of 18 and 21 are discharged from foster care each year. A national study prepared for the federal government reported that within two years after discharge, only 54% had completed high school, fewer than half were employed, 60% of the young women had given birth to a child, 25% had been homeless, and 30% were receiving public assistance.

Blanket exclusions throw away qualified parents, which we cannot afford to do. We don't know how many lesbians and gay men are adopting children, as no such statistics are kept. But we do know that each qualified lesbian or gay parent who is excluded because of his or her sexual orientation represents a potential loving family for a waiting child.

Under the governing child welfare policy across the country, no child is placed with an applicant unless, after a rigorous screening, a caseworker concludes that the applicant is the best match for the child. Excluding gay people (or any group) from being considered therefore does nothing whatsoever to protect children or promote good placements. All such exclusions do is prevent placement professionals from making some placements that they deem to be best for a particular child. Reducing the pool of available adoptive and foster parents from which caseworkers can choose provides no conceivable benefit to children and it creates harms that are all too real.

7

Gays and Lesbians Should Not Be Allowed to Adopt

Gary Glenn

Gary Glenn is president of the American Family Association of Michigan. He coauthored the Marriage Protection Amendment that Michigan voters approved in 2004.

While much was made of comedienne Rosie O'Donnell's announcement that she is a lesbian, very little attention has been paid to some starkly contradictory statements she made in an interview with Diane Sawyer. O'Donnell admitted that she thought her children's lives would be easier if she were married to a man, and that she hoped they would grow up to be heterosexual. These admissions exemplify the selfishness of gays and lesbians who adopt children to satisfy their own desires, despite overwhelming evidence that children's health is at greater risk when they are adopted into homosexual households. Studies have also shown that children of homosexual parents are much more likely to engage in homosexual behavior as adults, which carries with it extraordinary dangers to their physical and mental health. When children are placed in adopted homes, their welfare must be the first priority, not the political agenda of gay rights groups.

The media glorified [comedienne and talk show host] Rosie O'Donnell's public announcement that she has sex with other women. But it glossed over these startling contradictions: O'Donnell's frank admission that she believes her own

Gary Glenn, "Even Rosie Knows Homosexual Adoption Puts Children at Risk," www.cwfa.org, March 22, 2002. Reproduced by permission.

adopted children would be better off being raised by a married mother and father, bolstered by the hope that they won't follow her example of choosing to engage in homosexual behavior.

"Would it be easier for [my kids] if I were married to a man? It probably would," O'Donnell told ABC *Primetime Thursday* reporter Diane Sawyer [in 2002].

And when asked if she hopes her adopted children will grow up to be "straight." . . .

"Yes, I do," Rosie said. "I think life is easier if you're straight. . . . If I were to pick, would I rather have my children have to go through the struggles of being gay in America, or being heterosexual, I would say heterosexual."

Rosie also revealed that her six-year-old son Parker has told her, "I want to have a daddy." She responded, "If you were to have a daddy, you wouldn't have me as a mommy, because I'm the kind of mommy who wants another mommy. This is the way mommy got born."

Thus the biggest conclusion Americans should draw from the Rosie O'Donnell confessional is this—that Miss O'Donnell is a spoiled, privileged adult who put her own feelings ahead of what even she believes would be in the best interests of the children. She used her privilege and wealth to place children too young to object in an environment two recent studies indicate will make them *more likely* to engage in the very high risk behavior Rosie hopes they won't.

Putting Children in Danger

The scientific fact is that children's health is endangered if they are adopted into households in which the adults—as a direct consequence of their homosexual behavior—experience dramatically higher risks of domestic violence, mental illness, substance abuse, life-threatening disease, and premature death by up to 20 years.

- "The probability of violence occurring in a gay couple is mathematically *double* the probability of that in a heterosexual couple," write the editors of the National Gay & Lesbian Domestic Violence Network newsletter.

- *The Journal of the American Medical Association* reports that "people with same-sex sexual behavior are at greater risk for psychiatric disorders"—including bipolar, obsessive-compulsive, and anxiety disorders, major depression, and substance abuse.

- The Medical Institute of Sexual Health reports: "Homosexual men are at significantly increased risk of HIV/ AIDS, hepatitis, anal cancer, gonorrhea and gastrointestinal infections as a result of their sexual practices. Women who have sex with women are at significantly increased risk of bacterial vaginosis, breast cancer and ovarian cancer than are heterosexual women." (Executive Summary, "Health Implications Associated with Homosexuality," 1999.)

- The Institute reports that "significantly higher percentages of homosexual men and women abuse drugs, alcohol and tobacco than do heterosexuals."

- Oxford University's *International Journal of Epidemiology* reports: "Life expectancy at age 20 years for gay and bisexual men is 8 to 20 years less than for all men. . . . Nearly half of gay and bisexual men currently aged 20 years will not reach their 65th birthday."

Is it healthy for children to be adopted by adults whose lifestyle is characterized by promiscuity and the medical hazards of multiple sex partners?

- A homosexual newsmagazine columnist in Detroit last month [February 2002] wrote regarding his partner: "This is his first relationship, so he has not yet been ruined by all the heartache, lies, deceit, and game-playing that are the hallmark of gay relationships. . . . A study I once read suggested that *nine out of 10* gay men cheat on their lovers" [emphasis added].

- The Centers for Disease Control warns that men who have sex with men "have large numbers of anonymous partners, which can result in rapid, extensive transmission of sexually transmitted diseases."

Risk-Taking Adults

How will being adopted by adults involved in homosexual behavior affect the behavior of children themselves?

- *Associated Press* reported last June [2001] that a "new study by two University of Southern California sociologists says children with lesbian or gay parents . . . are probably *more likely to explore homosexual activity themselves* . . . (and) grow up to be more open to homoerotic relations." [emphasis added]

- A major Australian newspaper reported February 4 [2002] on a British sociologist's review of 144 academic papers on homosexual parenting: "Children raised by gay couples will suffer serious problems in later life, a study into parenting has found. The biggest investigation into same-sex parenting to be published in Europe claims children brought up by gay couples are *more likely to experiment with homosexual behavior* and be confused about their sexuality." [emphasis added]

Which means children adopted by adults involved in homosexual behavior face not only secondhand exposure to the risks of such behavior by their "parents," but are more likely to suffer firsthand by engaging in the same high-risk behavior themselves.

Young people who model the homosexual behavior of their adopted "parents" face other risks:

- *The Journal of the American Academy of Child & Adolescent Psychiatry* published a study of 4,000 high school students by Harvard Medical School, which found that "gay-lesbian-bisexual youth report disproportionate risk for a variety of health risk and problem behaviors . . . [from] engag[ing] in twice the mean number of risk behaviors as did the overall population." (Garofalo, Robert, *et al*, "The Association Between Health Risk Behaviors and Sexual Orientation Among a School-based Sample of Adolescents," *Pediatrics* 101, no. 5, May 1998: 895–902.)

- "GLB [gay, lesbian, bisexual] orientation was associated with increased . . . use of cocaine (and other illegal) drugs. GLB youth were more likely to report using tobacco, marijuana, and cocaine before 13 years of age. Among sexual risk behaviors, sexual intercourse before 13 years of age, sexual intercourse with four or more partners . . . and sexual contact against one's will all were associated with GLB orientation."

Child Welfare Before Politics

The sheer weight of evidence makes the issue clear: Should children be handed over as trophies to the homosexual "rights" movement—adopting them into households where they'll face dramatically higher risk of exposure to domestic violence, mental illness, life-threatening disease and premature death? An environment which increases the chances they'll engage in high-risk homosexual behavior themselves?

Not on your life, Rosie.

And certainly not theirs.

8

Father Registries Are Fair

Mardie Caldwell

Mardie Caldwell is the founder and chief executive officer of Lifetime Adoption Facilitation Center. She hosts the radio talk show Let's Talk Adoption *and has spoken about adoption in more than one hundred television appearances.*

Countless expectant women have run into a similar scenario where they wish to put their children up for adoption yet the birth fathers are either unwilling to consent to the adoption or cannot be found. Often these men will then refuse to provide assistance once the child is born, leaving the birth mother to support the child on her own. In fact, in many of these cases, the birth mother does have legal recourse to put the child up for adoption without the father's consent, but she is unaware of her power. We need laws that will save birth mothers from this heartache, and ensure that children are raised by parents who are able and willing to support them. Birth father registries need to be put in place around the country, to enable responsible fathers to claim responsibility for their children and, in the absences of such fathers, preserve birth mothers' rights to make decisions in their children's best interest. These registries would benefit all parties involved, resulting in less child abuse and dependency on welfare, and protecting the rights of caring, responsible fathers.

On average, 25 women call us [Lifetime Adoption Facilitation Center] each week, sharing one common concern: the requirement that the birth father consents and signs for the adoption. These women are desperately wanting to know how they can legally have their babies adopted if the father of their child has said he is not going to sign or is nowhere to be found. These men often have more than one woman pregnant at a time or have fathered other children they are not supporting emotionally or financially. They refuse to sign for the adoption yet will not provide any assistance in the form of financial or emotional help.

Thankfully, we know that there are also devoted birth fathers, interested in being part of an adoption plan and supporting the birth mother as she tries to make the right choices for her child. Some birth fathers have a true desire to parent their child, or at least support the child and mother financially. These are real fathers, fathers with a compassion and concern for the future of their child. And they are not the problem.

Birth fathers who stand in the way of what is best for the child, be it adoption or being a true father, are nothing more than "sperm donors." They just want to have a good time, then when a woman becomes pregnant and tries to do what is right in her mind by choosing adoption, he puts up a road block.

A woman in this position is fearful and often faced with a birth father that is simply not going to cooperate. Most of these men are not working, have a history of abuse or substance abuse, and have no intention of supporting the child. They want to know the "kid" is there if they want to see "it," some day, maybe someday, often never. They see kids from different women as trophies, validating they are able to produce, not realizing it takes so much more than sperm to be a Father and Dad to a child.

Women Facing Tough Decisions Alone

Frequently these women are burdened with three or more children, trying to raise them the best she can with never enough money, food, or support. Another mouth to feed would mean less for the children she has, and less hope of escaping the endless cycle she sees herself in. The fathers of her children are aware of the system and will make just enough money to support themselves, often working under the table to avoid having their paychecks garnished for child support. Three children, three different fathers and no form of child support—What is the mother to do with a baby that is due in a few weeks?

Naomi was one woman who didn't have the support of her family. At 21, she became pregnant with her third child. Once her parents and her boyfriend found out she was pregnant again, they shunned her. With no one offering guidance or help, she faced a tough decision alone.

Naomi said she considered placing her second child with an adoptive family, but decided to keep her baby when the birth father told her he wouldn't sign for the adoption, and her parents allowed her to move back in with them for a while.

"Everything was going fine until I found out I was pregnant again. Then everything let loose," she told me when she called, trying to make an adoption plan for the baby she was carrying. "Right now, it is the best decision I could make for all of us." She shared with me some of her daily difficulties, including struggling to keep the other children from running into the street.

Women are unaware of their power, and they buy into the fear these men put into their minds.

"When I told the father I was pregnant, he said it wasn't his. I haven't been with anyone else. I know it is his baby." She was asking how she can complete this adoption without his cooperation since he wouldn't even acknowledge it was his child. When we posed this question to an adoption attorney, we found that since they didn't live together he was only considered an alleged birth father. The lawyer would serve him papers, and if the time lapsed without a formal objection to the adoption, his rights would be terminated. Naomi could complete the adoption, placing her baby with the couple of her choice, without any recourse from him.

Strong Women Want More for Their Children

One of the reasons this country has so many children in foster care is that women are unaware of their power, and they buy into the fear these men put into their minds. We've had women tell us, "If I can't complete the adoption, I will just have an abortion. He can't stop me from that!"

We need laws that protect these children. When a woman is strong enough to go through with a pregnancy and wants to give her child a better life, she should have that choice. But because the man that fathered this child is unwilling to allow an adoption, the child, the mother, and her other children all suffer from this irresponsible man. We have found that most men like this are full of hot air; they have not completed anything in their lives, can't keep a job, may have outstanding warrants, and if they had to show up in court to contest the adoption, they would be arrested. So instead, they control and threaten to get the woman to keep a child they will not take any responsibility for.

If a birth father can see the benefit of adoption, an open adoption where there are choices, some will let the adoption go through without a fuss. Many logical men just want to be heard, they want to be part of the process, and not left out in the cold. They want some say and don't want to be judged.

These are the smart men that can think beyond themselves and what they can offer. These are real men that care for others and their children.

Open Adoption Offers So Much More

Adoption has changed and birth parents are given choices in adoption. An open adoption or semi-open adoption allows the birth parents to select a family for their child as well as updates and photos as the child grows if they wish.

Thirty years ago, a woman that was unable for whatever reason to parent her child could quietly go to a home and then place the child without having to get consent from the father. This was acceptable then when men fathering children out of wedlock was frowned upon.

In today's society it is common to have one, two or even three children by three different women. Only a small percentage of these men are responsible and willing to support their children, the others leave the task to an overburdened welfare system and the struggling women forced to raise another child, something she knows she hasn't the time, money, or strength to do.

New adoption laws need to be in place that allow responsible fathers to register with a "birth father registry."

Each week adoption professionals get calls from women seeking help, often with crying, screaming children in the background. It is any wonder that they have to go to desperate lengths to survive. Is this fair? Certainly not to the innocent children. A few will be lovingly placed for adoption in families that are eager and willing to provide a loving and stable home to a child.

Responsible Men Will Have Choices Also

These children need to grow up with parents that love them, committed to giving them the opportunities to be all they can be in life. New adoption laws need to be in place that allow responsible fathers to register with a "birth father registry," similar to the one used in Oregon and other states now. If a man knows he is the father of a child that is going to be born and wants to support the child, then he signs a registry acknowledging that he is the father and wants to be responsible. The fathers that do not sign the registry and are not interested in supporting the child then lose their rights. The mother can then choose what is best for her child, be it parenting or adoption.

When birth fathers do object to an adoption, 85% say they don't want the child placed because it will make them look bad. Their own macho image is more important to them than their child's future.

Everyone would benefit if we had in place more laws that required men to register.

No wonder we have so many women forced into not naming the father, saying they were raped, or claiming that they sleep around, just so that they can give their child a better life. Can you blame a woman that makes this choice? She is reaching out for help, wanting to do something that she feels is in the best interest of her child, and wanting to insure that her child has a true father, not this loser who places more worth on his image than his child. It's a simple fact that when children grow up, they will often mirror the behaviors of their own father or mother. And so, without better choices made, the negative cycle continues.

Breaking the Cycle of Abuse and Poverty

If a little girl sees her mother abused, then she will often be attracted to men in her life that will treat her as her mother was treated. The mothers that call us are trying to stop this cycle. They are bright women that want more for their children. They see what they are not able to provide now, and know that they want more for their child, in spite of the personal sacrifice. Women with this much love and concern for their children should not be forced to parent or to abandon their baby in an alley, in hopes it will be found.

Everyone would benefit if we had in place more laws that required men to register. We would see less child abuse, less women dependent on welfare for their support. It would allow the responsible men to have their rights upheld and the irresponsible ones granted no rights unless they take the steps themselves needed to raise these little ones. It would give thousands of children the basics in life that they don't have, or don't have any hope of receiving. And most importantly, it would offer every child the hope for a safe home and the promise of a future.

No one will deny that we have too many children entering the foster care system every day. Many of these children could have been placed for adoption at birth or a younger age and given a chance for a safe adoptive home and a loving forever family, something that many of their mothers had hoped for before they took their first breath. Reach out in your community, speak to the lawmakers and representatives that can help change the adoption laws. And maybe, just maybe, the next generation will have a chance at a better life.

9

Father Registries Are Not Fair

Jane Spies and Murray Davis

Jane Spies is executive director and a cofounder of the National Family Justice Association. Murray Davis is board president and cofounder of the National Family Justice Association.

The rights of biological parents to care for their own children have recently come under attack, as exemplified by the case of Mark Huddleston, whose son was placed with an adoptive couple without his consent. Despite going through all possible legal channels, Huddleston still does not have custody of his son. While such cases are common, the American public knows little about their prevalence. When these cases are reported, fathers like Huddleston are commonly portrayed as deadbeat dads who needlessly stand in the way of adoptions. One response to situations like Huddleston's has been the formation of putative father registries that require potential fathers to sign a state registry in order to be informed if their child is put up for adoption. These registries devalue fathers and the roles they play in their children's lives. Furthermore, they are so scarcely advertised that few men are aware of their existence. Even when men do put their names on the registry, their rights to their children are not always protected. The creation of putative father registries may be motivated by the economic interests of the adoption industry, rather than the well-being of the children. In place of these registries, it should be required that a birth mother reveal the names of any potential fathers before an adoption goes through. This will protect the rights of both parents, and in the process, the welfare of the child.

Jane Spies and Murray Davis, "A Father's Love Denied: Adoption Gone Wrong," *National Family Justice Association*, July 20, 2005. Reproduced by permission.

The negative implications of the recent [June 23, 2005] controversial U.S. Supreme Court *Kelo v. New London* eminent domain decision ruling that government could transfer private property, in that case a home to a private corporation since more tax revenue would be generated are still reverberating throughout our country . . . and rightly so.

But far more precious rights are being "stolen," to put it mildly, and they have been for years. We speak of fundamental Constitutional rights and the liberty interest of fit biological parents to the care, custody, and control of their own biological children.

Consider the story of Mark Huddleston, married father of 2 grown children, recently covered by the Associated Press (6/14/05):

Mark Huddleston is doing everything within his power to stay in his beloved 16-month-old biological son's life and to raise him, to no avail, so far.

According to the *Albuquerque Journal* (6/14/05), in March 2005, a judge terminated Mark Huddleston's parental rights to his biological son with no visitation. Mark has appealed that decision. It is reported that a private adoption agency had placed Mark's son with a prospective adoptive couple 3 days after his birth, without Mark's consent to an adoption. Huddleston first learned of his son's birth when he received a letter from that adoption agency, Adoptions Plus, in April 2004, informing him of the possibility that he might have a 2-month-old child.

Mark Huddleston said, "As soon as I heard of my son's birth, I immediately went to the adoption agency to let them know that if this is my child, I will not consent to an adoption. I feel like I'm in another country. I thought this kind of thing just can't happen in America. I just want my son."

Huddleston's Struggle Continues

According to news reports, in December of 2004, Mark had been given supervised visitation with his son, pending the custody trial that he filed in April 2004, immediately after learning of his child's birth.

He met his son for the very first time when the baby was 11 months old. "Huddleston said his child reached for him the first day they met. 'I don't know if it's genetic bonding or what,' he said."

One would think that common sense would dictate the immediate return of the son to his biological father.

It was reported that even the state of New Mexico said Mark should have the opportunity to raise the child since ". . . the private adoption agency hadn't properly notified Huddleston. . . ."

Despite the state's statement in his favor and Mark's outstanding perseverance in trying to obtain custody of his own child—he has spent $70,000 on legal proceedings to gain custody, so far—Mark still does not have his son.

Why not?

One would think that common sense would dictate the immediate return of the son to his biological father. Furthermore, public opinion is overwhelmingly on Mark's side, as evidenced by reported audience reaction to a radio talk show interview of Mark in June 2005.

We at the National Family Justice Association (NFJA) believe this blatant injustice to Mark's family and other similarly situated families should be front-page daily news.

Perhaps part of the reason for the lack of adequate public attention to the unjust loss of fit parents' parental rights is that this potential loss of such fundamental rights is just too terrible to imagine. But as we, a nation, are now facing the potential negative implications of the "Kelo decision" to individual property rights, we must now face the implications of years of ignoring basic constitutional protections for natural fit parents of the care, custody, and control of our own children.

Many Similar Stories

NFJA wants to raise public awareness of the issue of adoptions gone awry so that just and proper solutions can be found. Tragically, there are many similar stories where fit and loving biological fathers lose children against their will.

Frequently, dads who come forward to assert their paternity to prevent an adoption are not welcomed, or are not seen as loving, aggrieved dads. Rather, they are too often seen as "troublemakers" or obstacles to closing an adoption deal. Their suffering, and the suffering of their extended families, including grandparents, over the loss of beloved children is unacknowledged or denied.

For example [according to a 2000 story in the *Guardian*]:

> In New York, a 20-year-old father lost his son to an adoption that was finalized without this dad's consent and against his wishes. The mother of his son and the baby's grandmother had concealed the existence of the baby from him. He only learned this after the grandmother apparently relented and decided to tell him that there was indeed a child who had been adopted away from him. By then, his son was 13 months old.

Various ways have been proposed to address how to avoid situations where birth fathers come forward to claim their children who have been adopted out against their will, without their knowledge, or without their consent. One "solution" is the implementation of "putative father registries," which we believe are being used in about 25 states.

Registry Is Unfair to Fathers

Although state requirements and procedures vary, in general, a man who has sexual relations that might result in a pregnancy must sign up with the state within varying periods of time of the child's birth, or before the birth, to be notified that an adoption might be pending. The man must give his name and the prospective mother's name or other information, depending upon state requirements, so that he can be notified if an adoption petition is filed.

We believe that the putative father registry idea, as it now stands, devalues fathers and fatherhood. Are fathers considered so unimportant or disposable that their rights to their own offspring are protected only by a tenuous system that seems to be untested, unevaluated, ineffective, and virtually unadvertised?

Did you ever hear of the putative father registry and do you know what is required for unmarried dads to claim their biological children? We believe that most readers would say that they have not heard of such a registry.

And we cannot possibly understand how putting a woman's and man's name on a "putative father registry list"— even though we're assured it's confidential—protects the mom's or dad's privacy.

Furthermore, do the putative father registries really "work"? Apparently it didn't work for one Ohio dad who signed the state registry, as required. An alleged "computer error" prevented the putative father registry system from notifying this dad of the pending adoption of his son by an Ohio couple.

And what if an adoption is filed outside of the state in which the "putative father" registered? According to *The Cincinnati Enquirer*, 3/23/03, an Indiana dad signed the Indiana registry as required but still lost rights to his baby daughter, "Baby Colette," who had been taken to another state and put up for adoption without his knowledge and against his will.

There is talk of implementing a national putative father registry, but the aforementioned questions would still apply.

Motives Behind Registry

We should ask ourselves why we as a society are trying to come up with such a circuitous way, perhaps prone to failure, to inform prospective dads of a pregnancy or birth of a child. Why are some making it so difficult for fathers to raise their own children? Might it have something to do with monetary interests of the adoption industry and ensuring that there is an ample "supply" of adoptable children? Adoption can be expensive.

For example, "Adoption can cost $15,000 to $20,000 or even more, but credits, reimbursements, and other benefits can make your adoption affordable. . . ."

The solution is really simple. Birth mothers should be required to disclose the names of all potential fathers, with paternity established by DNA testing, prior to legalizing all adoptions.

Adoptions . . . must be done with proper notice and due process rights for both biological parents.

There are many ways to locate people if one makes an earnest and diligent effort to do so. We believe that a dad, facing the adoption of his child against his will, must have legal notice and due process. It can't just be an ad in an obscure newspaper in another state or a letter sent to his last known address. This isn't merely notice of an overdue parking ticket that we are talking about. This is far more serious. This involves a parent's life with his or her child, and should be treated as such.

Registry Hurts Children

Every child has the right to know his or her own parents and genetic medical history. We can't simply say to fit biological parents opposing an adoption and who want their child: "Yes, you're fit, but we found 2 other 'fitter' parents who can offer something better to your child." This is not how our system is supposed to work. The private realm of family should not be intruded upon in this egregious way.

We believe you can't separate a child's right from a fit parent's rights. If you thwart a parent's rights, you indirectly hurt the child. A fit parent, mom or dad, protects their child by virtue of his or her parental rights. They are the people best situated to know what their child needs. They are the ones who know what is truly in their child's best interest. We believe the rights of the child include preserving the child's fit biological parents' rights, until and unless those rights are willingly, legally, and knowingly given up.

We are certainly not against adoptions, but it must be done with proper notice and due process rights for both biological parents, not under duress, with informed consent, and preferably openly so that adoptees can know their parentage in the future. All person's interests, including the interests of the prospective adoptive parents, would then be protected.

Prioritize Parental Rights and Child Welfare

The monetary interests of adoption agencies or others with vested interests in a thriving adoption "industry" should not supersede our basic fundamental rights to our own children and children's rights to their parents. We fear that financial interests are now too much in the foreground, while, too often, biological parents' rights are ignored to further commercial financial interests.

In recent years, the oft-repeated government public service announcement tag line, which apparently was meant to encourage so-called "irresponsible fathers" to "become responsible" was: "They're your kids, be their dad."

We cringe when we hear that phrase because most fathers are indeed responsible, and they want to be there to love and raise their children, as does any good parent. This phrase reinforces and perpetuates an erroneous and damaging negative stereotype of the "runaway" or "absent" dad. The stereotype denies the reality that there are countless deadbolted, noncustodial dads and moms, unfairly and unnecessarily locked out of their children's lives with little or no recourse to get back in.

Mark's case illustrates the phenomenon of the "deadbolted dad" well. He did what society says it wants dads to do. . . . He stepped up for his beloved son. Yet he's still waiting and actively seeking to have his child. Every day that passes is precious time forever lost between this dad and his son.

The bottom line is this: Children need and love their fathers equally as much as they need and love their mothers. Fathers love their children equally as much as mothers do. Fathers do matter—yes, including unmarried fathers.

10

Single People Should Be Given the Same Opportunity as Couples to Adopt

Amanda J. Crawford

Amanda J. Crawford is a reporter for the Arizona Republic *in Phoenix, AZ.*

A bill that has passed the Arizona House and is expected to pass the state Senate would require the state's Department of Economic Security (DES) to place adoptive children with married couples before single people, except in specific situations. The bill is intended to strengthen support for the nuclear family at a time when alternative family structures are growing in number. The DES and many child advocates and adoption agencies oppose the bill, arguing that there are close to three hundred Arizona children waiting for homes and the bill will discourage potential single parents from adopting.

As she recovered from breast cancer five years ago, Roz Merkle took stock of her life.

She was nearly 50. She had divorced and raised two boys on her own. Now, her sons were grown. And Merkle still had love to give.

"I started thinking about what I wanted to do, and I knew I wanted to adopt," she said.

Merkle, who had been adopted as an infant, decided to take in teenagers, usually the most difficult children for the

Amanda J. Crawford, "Adoption Bill Hurts Singles, Kids, Critics Say," *Arizona Republic*, April 13, 2006. Reproduced by permission.

state to place in homes. And now she has two teenage girls, offering them sanctuary, because they had been abused, and a strong female role model.

But a bill expected to be passed by the [Arizona] state Senate would put potential parents like Merkle at the end of the line. The measure, which was approved by the House in March [2006] and given preliminary approval in the Senate last week [April 2006], would force the state Department of Economic Security [DES] to place children with married couples first, except in specific circumstances.

If the measure passes the Senate and is signed by the governor, the state would have to show that there are no qualified married couples or prove in court that it was in the "best interest" of the child, one of the other exceptions in the law, to place a child with a single person.

The bill, opposed by DES and child advocates, is raising questions about the nature of family at a time when cultural perceptions of family, marriage and parenthood are in flux with more single-parent, unmarried and same-sex households than ever.

The measure seeks to combat, in part, the state's endorsement of those alternative family arrangements by placing the preference for a traditional, nuclear family in state law for children in state custody. "Regardless of those debates of what a family should be, adoption law has always considered married mothers and fathers are best for a child," said Peter Gentala, legal counsel for the conservative Center for Arizona Policy. Gentala helped draft the measure.

There are close to 300 children in state custody waiting for adoptive families.

This bill says "we are not going to get away from that even as there are more and more voices who would shift it away." "I believe the widespread belief among most Americans and Arizonans is that children should have a mom and a dad."

Opposition to the Bill

DES, adoption agencies, children advocates and single parents have come out against the bill. They say they fear it would discourage single people from volunteering to adopt children in need at a time when there are close to 300 children in state custody waiting for adoptive families and new children entering the system every day. They also say they fear the bill would restrict the decision process, now based on the needs of individual children, and lengthen the court process to complete the adoptions.

Gay rights groups have also come out against the bill. Some opponents say they believe that barring adoption by gay couples, who must adopt as a single person, is the hush-hush motivation behind the measure.

Sen. Karen Johnson, head of the Senate Family Services Committee and a supporter of the bill, denies that blocking gay adoptions is the motivation. She says she and other supporters simply believe that children do better with both a mom and a dad.

"It is in the best interest of the child," Johnson said.

Now, when DES workers choose placement for a child in state custody, they weigh many factors to find the right home for each child. Whether there is a mom and a dad at home can be part of the placement decision, as are numerous other factors, but it is not always priority No. 1.

Some children may do better in a traditional home. But other factors may be more important for some children, opponents of the measure say.

"The difference is you are taking the human element out of it and you are prioritizing it based on a blanket rule and a belief system," said Ron Adelson, executive director of Aid to Adoption of Special Kids, which helps to find foster and adoptive homes to children in state custody. "We have a lot of single parents who have come forward. Many of them have been great."

A Chilling Effect

Already, most state adoptions are with married couples. In the past 12 months, there have been about 1,000 finalized adoptions of children in state custody. Only 220 of them were single-parent adoptions.

DES spokeswoman Liz Barker said the agency believes it needs to keep the door open to all applicants to be able to have choices so it can find the right home for a child.

The measure would make it "kind of like a child being put on an auction block."

"We are concerned about the message it sends: that single people need not apply," she said.

The bill's sponsor, Rep. Steve Tully, said he does not understand why his "innocuous" bill has caused so much controversy. But he declined to return calls for further comment.

When the Senate considered the bill for preliminary approval, Democratic Sens. Jorge Garcia and Rebecca Rios offered several unsuccessful amendments, some likely tongue-in-cheek, that would have replaced the preference for married couples with other possible considerations. The amendments included preference for people who have been baptized, who have health insurance, who are of the same ethnicity as the child or who live in the same school district.

Merkle, of north Phoenix, said she understands the controversy and believes DES needs to have flexibility to find the right family for each child, whether that means a mom and a dad or just a mom, like her.

"We just need to give these kids good, loving homes," she said. The measure would make it "kind of like a child being put on an auction block, and if married people don't bid on her, we'll give her to a single person. I think it should be judged by individual cases."

11

China's New Adoption Restrictions Are Not Fair

Beth Nonte Russell

Beth Nonte Russell is the author of Forever Lily: An Unexpected Mother's Journey to Adoption in China *and the founder of Big Mind Publishing.*

China has just announced a stricter set of guidelines for parents of other nations interested in adopting Chinese babies, in spite of a reported decline in international adoptions from China in the past year. Chinese officials are allegedly concerned about the current ratio of boys to girls, yet there still appears to be an overwhelming number of girls in orphanages. It seems that China is more concerned with its image than the welfare of its children. When it puts an end to its international adoption program, China's reason should be because there are no more babies to be adopted and not as an attempt to improve its reputation. If China's demand does indeed outweigh its supply of orphaned children, it should make these numbers public.

According to a State Department report released [in January 2007], American citizens adopted 6,493 children from China in 2006, a decline of 18 percent from the previous year's total of 7,906. And yet . . . [in December 2006], this newspaper [the *New York Times*] reported that China had prepared strict new criteria for foreign adoption applications because the country claimed it lacked "available" babies to meet the "spike" in demand.

China has always limited foreign adoptions, and it does not publish reliable statistics on the number of children in its orphanages. So how is one to know whether the decrease in adoptions reflects a lack of supply or a lack of demand?

In the week following the report on the new guidelines, more than one bewildered person said to me, "But I thought there were lots of babies in orphanages in China!" My response was to helplessly reply, "So did I." My understanding of this was based not on conjecture, but on having been to China twice to adopt, having seen orphanages with my own eyes, and on research and other eyewitness accounts. Many hundreds and perhaps thousands of orphanages operate in China, most of them full of girls.

National pride is more important than getting these children into loving homes.

"Missing" Girls

According to a February 2005 report in *The Weekend Standard*, a Chinese business newspaper, demographers in China found a ratio of 117 boys per 100 girls under the age of 5 in the 2000 census. Thanks to China's one-child policy, put into effect in 1979 in order to curb population growth, and a strong cultural preference for male children, this gender gap could result in as many as 60 million "missing" girls from the population by the end of the decade, enough to alarm even Chinese officials.

And what happened to these girls? According to the International Planned Parenthood Federation (a term that takes on a whole new meaning when referring to China), there are about seven million abortions in China per year, 70 percent of which are estimated to be of females. That adds up to around five million per year, or 50 million by the end of the decade; so where are the other 10 million girls? If even 10 percent end up in orphanages well, you do the math.

A few months ago, in a conversation with my friend Patrick Mason, executive director of the International Adoption Center at INOVA Fairfax Hospital in Virginia, I confessed a growing fear: that China, the country from which my two daughters were adopted, would sooner or later shut down its international adoption program Dr. Mason immediately dismissed my concern, saying, "The number of orphans is just too great."

National Priorities

And yet, I continued to wonder whether, as China increasingly asserts itself on the world stage and prepares to host the 2008 Summer Olympics, allowing Westerners to adopt thousands of infants each year would fit the image it wanted to project. I suspect not, and China's new restrictions lead me to believe that national pride is more important than getting these children into loving homes.

The issue of abandoned and institutionalized children remains a taboo subject in China, a problem the government does not even acknowledge exists. The impulse to hide it seems to stem partly from embarrassment and partly from fear of revealing the grave human rights abuses the one-child policy has produced; surely, watching a parade of well-off foreigners cart off thousands of babies would make the Chinese authorities understandably uncomfortable.

But the answer is not to stop the foreigners from adopting; it is to put an end to their reasons for doing so. My fondest hope, and the hope of thousands of parents who have adopted from China, is for all the orphanages there to close because there are no more abandoned children to put in them. This will be accomplished only when China decides that there is no economic or political justification for the magnitude of suffering that has resulted from the one-child policy. The government must openly acknowledge the problem, in part by publishing verifiable information about the status of its orphaned children, and take real steps to correct it. To do so would go a long way toward building the international trust and respect China seems to want so badly.

Looking for Answers

China has announced the lifting of restrictions for foreign journalists in preparation for the 2008 Olympics. Perhaps this will allow reporters to look for answers to some basic questions: how many children are there in institutions in China? If there is nothing to hide, why do visitors need approval to visit orphanages? Why are only certain orphanages allowed to participate in the international adoption program, and what is going on in the ones that are not?

The Hague Convention on Intercountry Adoption, to which China and 69 other countries are signatories, goes a long way toward ensuring against child abduction and trafficking; but it does not include provisions that would require member countries to report such information as the number of children housed in institutions or the criteria used for selecting "suitable" children for adoption.

Madonna is still eligible, at least until she turns 50, gets fat . . . , gets divorced or goes broke.

The treaty states that "for the full and harmonious development of his or her personality," each child should have the opportunity to grow up in a "family environment, in an atmosphere of happiness, love and understanding." Indeed, it requires that each signatory take "as a matter of priority, appropriate measures to enable the child to remain in the care of his or her family of origin." One could argue that China's one-child policy directly violates the treaty by ensuring that many children will not remain in the care of the family but be relinquished to the care of the state.

Who Is Excluded?

Under the new Chinese adoption guidelines, the international adoption celebrity Angelina Jolie could not adopt from China (she's not married, and alas, and she and Brad [Pitt] have more than two divorces between them, which is a no-no); nor could the actress Meg Ryan (again, not married). Another person who is not eligible is yours truly. My husband is over 50, so I would have to trade him in, marry again, wait the required five years (another new rule) before beginning the adoption process, and by that time I would be sneaking up on 50 myself.

It is comforting to know that Madonna is still eligible, at least until she turns 50, gets fat (the new regulations call for a body mass index of less than 40), gets divorced or goes broke (anyone with a net worth of under $80,000 is excluded).

The Chinese have asserted that the demand for adoptions far exceeds the number of babies it deems "available," based on criteria that have never been made public. We can only wonder how many babies will be left behind by Beijing's new policies—perhaps spending their lives in institutions because of these arbitrary and artificial limits.

12

The U.S. Government Should Strengthen Regulations on International Adoptions

Cindy Freidmutter

Cindy Freidmutter is the former executive director of the Evan B. Donaldson Adoption Institute. She is currently vice president for External and Community Affairs at LaGuardia Community College in New York.

The Evan B. Donaldson Adoption Institute, which I represent, urges the State Department to revise the current regulations on international adoptions. These regulations, as they stand, are insufficient in protecting children, birth parents, and adoptive parents from dangerous market forces. There are three critical issues that must be addressed in the Intercountry Adoption Act (IAA). First, U.S. adoption agencies should facilitate all financial transactions between adoptive families and service providers abroad. Second, American adoption agencies should provide adoptive families with clear and comprehensive contracts that protect these families. Third, American families considering international adoption should have objective information about adoption providers available to them. If the State Department would implement these and other changes to the international adoption regulations, it would make considerable strides toward improving the American experience with, and outlook on, international adoption.

Cindy Freidmutter, "International Adoptions: Problems and Solutions," before the House Committee on International Relations, Committee on International Relations, May 22, 2002.

Thank you for inviting me to testify about how the federal government can effectively implement the Hague Convention and the Intercountry Adoption Act (IAA) to improve international adoption services for adoptive families, birth parents and adopted children and ensure a more ethical adoption environment internationally. I represent the Evan B. Donaldson Adoption Institute (Adoption Institute), a not-for-profit national policy and research organization devoted to improving the quality of adoption policy and practice, and the public's perception of adoption. Throughout the regulatory drafting process, the Adoption Institute has advocated that the State Department tailor the regulations to address the most serious problems with international adoption. Unfortunately, the current draft regulations will not fulfill a primary purpose of the IAA—"protect[ing] the rights of, and prevent[ing] abuses against children, birth families, and adoptive parents involved in adoption."

International adoption has evolved into a potentially lucrative and largely unregulated business. Over the last decade, the number of international adoptions by Americans has increased threefold from about 6,500 in 1992 to over 19,000 in 2001. Accurate information is not currently compiled by any reliable source about the aggregate fees charged for international adoption services. One can reasonably estimate, however, that U.S. adoptive parents spent close to $200 million in 2001 for international adoption services. As the number of international adoptions has grown, there has been a corresponding sharp escalation in the number of individuals and agencies, here and abroad, involved in facilitating the adoption process. In 1989, only a handful of adoptions took place in Russia and China, but by 2001, these two countries accounted for nearly half of all international adoptions by Americans. By the end of the 1990s, there were 80 U.S. agencies active in Russia and 150 active in China. The market forces inherent in international adoption pose a potential threat to the welfare of children, as well as their birth parents and prospective adoptive parents.

Evidence and experience highlight three critical issues with international adoption services provided in the United States, which the Adoption Institute urges the State Department to address in the IAA regulations.

Document All Monetary Transactions

First U.S. providers should be directly responsible for all financial transactions with and payments to their contractors and agents in other countries, and should be accountable to families who rely on their representations about fees.

U.S. families who adopt internationally are generally told by their agencies to carry substantial amounts of cash abroad to pay fees, a dangerous and sometimes illegal practice. A recent Adoption Institute survey of over 1,600 American families who adopted internationally through U.S. agencies found that three out of four families were required by their agencies to carry cash to their adoptive child's country of origin to pay adoption service fees, with most directed to bring $3,000 or more. And 11% of all respondents stated that when they were overseas, agency facilitators asked them to pay additional fees that were not disclosed by the agencies.

Currently, U.S. families adopting internationally are not afforded basic consumer legal protections.

It is logical to presume that undocumented cash transactions by American adoptive families are a major factor in fostering unethical practices overseas. The current draft regulations, however, will not curb this practice by only requiring "an official and recorded means of fund transfer, whenever possible." In order to reduce financial incentives that may lead to illegal and unethical practices, financial transactions must be transparent and recorded. IAA regulations should require providers to develop an official and recorded means of fund transfer, unless the State Department issues a written determination that it is not possible to do so in a specific country.

Make Contracts Comprehensive

Second, adoption service contracts between providers and prospective adoptive families should create a clear predictable business relationship by enumerating in plain language the services to be provided, the fees to be paid, the legal responsibility of the adoption agencies for staff, agents and subcontractors, the complaint resolution processes and other critical information.

Currently, U.S. families adopting internationally are not afforded basic consumer legal protections. While many parents who adopt internationally sign a contract with their adoption agencies, these "contracts" too often fail to create a fair and clear business relationship with respect to services, fees and legal responsibility. Consequently, families have no recourse when agencies do not provide promised services, give them inaccurate information, or increase the fees while the adoption is in process, problems which happen to a significant minority of families.

Of the 1,600 families who responded to the Adoption Institute's survey,

- 15% reported that their agency withheld information or told them inaccurate information about the child,

- Another 15% said their agency withheld information or told them inaccurate information about the adoption process, and

- 14% said their adoption cost more than the agency told them it would cost.

The regulations should specify the type of information that must be included in adoption service contracts. Contracts protect parents and providers alike, providing clarity about the parties' respective roles and responsibilities, and guidance to courts in the event of disputes. While the draft regulations require providers to disclose "fully and in writing" their policies and practices, inexplicably they do not mandate that providers include that information in adoption service contracts. Similarly, the draft regulations require that some, but not all, fee information be disclosed in contracts. The bottom line is that prospective adoptive parents should not have to comb through the Code of Federal Regulations to insure that their agencies are providing legally required information and services at agreed-upon fees.

Provide More Information

Third, prospective adoptive parents should have access to objective information to guide their choice of international adoption service providers.

One of the simplest and most effective ways of accomplishing a primary purpose of the IAA—"prevent[ing] abuses against . . . adoptive parents"—is to provide them with the information they need to make informed choices about providers. Information about service quality and provider performance would likely enhance prospective adoptive parents' ability to make educated decisions, thereby improving their satisfaction rates. Currently, a significant minority of parents who responded to the Adoption Institute survey were not happy with their agencies' performance:

- 13% were not satisfied with the services they received from adoption agencies.

- 14% would not recommend their agency to other families.

The draft regulations do not address consumer education in an effective manner. There is no requirement that an independent entity publish comparable performance information that would help prospective adoptive families make informed choices. Publication of such information would also create a strong incentive for "weaker" providers to improve service quality and performance. The regulations should mandate that service quality and outcome data generated by the accreditation process be used to educate prospective adoptive families about provider performance in the following ways:

- Publication of a consumer handbook explaining the regulation of providers, and accreditation and complaint processes,

- Creation of an annual consumer report card, available on the Internet and in print, that evaluates providers' compliance with the regulations and key quality indicators, and

- Providing access on the Internet and in print to provider-specific comparable service quality, performance and cost information.

Other Strategies for Improvement

The Adoption Institute has also recommended that the State Department adopt the following additional strategies to fundamentally improve the quality of international adoption practice. By incorporating these proposals into the regulations, the Adoption Institute believes that the federal government will dramatically improve actual experience with and public perception of international adoption.

- Identify poor quality providers in a timely manner, and create a regulatory enforcement climate where they either meet standards or lose accreditation.

- Require providers to be legally responsible to the families who contract with them for acts of their agents and contractors in the United States and abroad.

- Mandate that providers carry liability insurance that reflects the risk of work conducted by all its agents and contractors.

- Ensure prospective adoptive families receive access to the best available information about referred children.

- Guarantee adopted persons and their families access to their adoption records to the fullest extent permitted by the Hague Convention and IAA.

- Create an Ombudsman or similar independent entity that enables families engaged in international adoption to report and resolve complaints involving providers' regulatory noncompliance. An Ombudsman would also:

- Provide consumer education about the complaint process.

- Facilitate timely resolution of consumer complaints.

- Routinely analyze complaint patterns and outcome data to identify providers that are in violation of regulatory standards.

- Advise Congress and the State Department about ongoing problems, and the impact of the regulations and accreditation process on improving service quality.

I appreciate the opportunity to share the Adoption Institute's perspective on improving international adoption services.

13

The Interstate Compact on the Placement of Children Should Be Reformed

Liz Oppenheim

Liz Oppenheim is the director of Interstate Affairs at the American Public Human Services Association (APHSA) and oversees the management of the Interstate Compact on Adoption and Medical Assistance (ICAMA).

The Interstate Compact on the Placement of Children (ICPC) has recently come under some scrutiny. While the ICPC plays a vital role in the appropriate placement of children, many professionals in the child welfare field are dissatisfied with the current version of the compact, complaining that it unnecessarily delays the placement of children. The compact uses overly broad language to define itself and its scope, lacks proper enforcement and accountability, and prescribes procedures that are incompatible with today's children's needs. For instance, the ICPC was originally written based on the premise that all states send and receive the same number of children. But today, this assumption no longer holds; in fact, many states send far more children than they receive, and vice versa. The result is that the distribution of resources among states is disproportionate to the needs of those states, so that many states do not have the resources they require. The ICPC's mandates for the court system also add unnecessary complexity and delay in many cases. These outdated procedures, as well as other weaknesses in the current compact, necessitate

Liz Oppenheim, "Re-Forming the Interstate Compact on the Placement of Children," *National Center for Interstate Compacts Connections*, Winter 2005. Reproduced by permission.

the reform of the ICPC so that it may better respond to the circumstances and needs of today's children and adoptive families.

Renewed focus on safety and permanency for children in the United States child welfare system has brought the Interstate Compact on the Placement of Children (ICPC) into the spotlight. While this attention confirmed the important role the ICPC plays in ensuring appropriate placements, it has also highlighted concerns that the ICPC processes cause unnecessary delays. States and other child welfare professionals have become increasingly dissatisfied with the ICPC as it is currently written and implemented. Some of the problems with the current compact include: (1) its overly broad language in terms of the definition and scope, (2) its inadequate procedures in addressing the needs of today's children, and (3) the current structure's lack of enforcement and accountability. In short, the ICPC is outdated for 21st century child welfare practice.

The current ICPC was drafted in 1960 and has been enacted by all states, the District of Columbia and the U.S. Virgin Islands. It ensures protection and services to children placed across state lines for foster care or adoption by establishing procedures that ensure placements are safe, suitable and able to provide proper care. It also assigns legal and financial responsibilities to those involved in making the placements.

The ICPC process entails a thorough home study conducted by the receiving state. This involves assessments of social and medical histories of the placement family, their backgrounds, parenting and discipline styles, employment and financial histories, physical evaluation of their home, criminal and child abuse background checks, personal and professional references, foster or adoptive parent training, and case worker recommendations. Once the placement is determined to be "not contrary to the welfare of the child" and the child is placed, the receiving state is responsible for ongoing supervision of the placement and for providing support services to the family and child and regular reports to the sending state agency and court. In addition, sending and receiving states must reach agreement on how services and supports will be financed. This can be complex because it involves the cooperation of several systems in both states, including education and mental health.

Complexities in the ICPC

Over its 44-year history and due to the broad scope of the compact's language, the ICPC has come to include many populations of children. The compact currently covers foster children placed with a relative or other caregiver, children moving across state lines with their foster parents, children placed for adoption by a public or private agency or by a private attorney, children placed in residential treatment facilities by parents, parents placing children with non-relatives, and pregnant mothers who cross state lines to give birth and place their child for adoption.

The ICPC was formulated on the assumption that each state would send the same number of children as they received. Therefore, the financial burden to states of conducting home studies and providing post-placement supervision for children placed in their states would be offset by the similar costs borne by other states. However, data and anecdotal evidence show that today many states send more children than they receive, and some states receive many more children than they send. This disproportion has compromised the ability of some states to provide the necessary resources for home studies and ongoing supervision. Adding to the demand on states' resources is the fact that concurrent planning requires case workers to make multiple home study requests for one child. Each home study must be financed, but placement can occur with only one of the families studied.

The court system adds another layer of complexity. A child cannot be removed from his home or placed in a foster or adoptive home without a judge's approval. Courts must ensure that reasonable efforts have been made to reunify a child with birth parents before a petition can be filed for termination of parental rights. They also must ensure that prospective adoptive parents are appropriate during an official waiting period of between three and 12 months before rendering a final decision.

Many of the factors that complicate the ICPC process underline struggles in the overall child welfare system, which continually contends with capacity, staffing, training and resource issues.

Interstate Placements Today and In the Future

Interstate placements are on the rise and are expected to continue to grow as relative placements and geographic barriers to adoption fade. A significant component of states' efforts to increase permanency and adoption for children in the child welfare system is the recognition that resource families for the children who need homes can be located anywhere in the United States. With the launch of the AdoptUSKids web site and national recruitment campaign, states now have a vehicle that allows them to find prospective adoptive families from across the nation for waiting children. As of Sept. 30, 2001, 542,000 children in out-of-home placements, (60 percent) will be reunified with birth parents: The remaining will need permanent families. Most will be placed in homes close to their communities; for others, the most appropriate placement may be with a family in another state. Interstate placements offer a greater chance of adoption to children who may be difficult to place, since resource families from all states can be accessed and made aware of their need.

Data from the Adoption and Foster Care Analysis Reporting System (AFCARS) show that nationwide, the annual number of completed adoptions from foster care doubled between 1995 and 2000. Researchers expect the rate of growth in adoption from foster care will exceed the rate of growth of the foster care population for at least the next two decades.

Although adoptions have increased substantially, at any given time about 8,000 children are waiting to be adopted but have no immediate adoption prospects.

To improve the interstate placement process, true reform require[s] revisions to the actual language of the ICPC itself.

Currently [in 2005], interstate placements constitute about 5.5 percent of children served in foster care annually, and some 4 percent in care on any given day. The largest proportion of the children placed through the ICPC—about 40 percent—are placed with relatives in other states. This significantly exceeds the national figures showing that relatives care for 25 percent of all children in foster care. Moreover, children who are placed interstate are twice as likely to be placed in pre-adoptive homes as in-state children. In fact, data show that two-thirds of children placed in another state are adopted by the families with whom they were placed.

Rewriting the ICPC

In March 2004, the American Public Human Services Association's (APHSA) state human services leadership adopted a policy resolution directing a rewrite of the ICPC. While the association members agreed that there are a number of interim steps that can be taken to improve the interstate placement process, true reform required revisions to the actual language of the ICPC itself. APHSA, in response to this resolution, assembled a development and drafting team composed of a diverse group of state human service administrators, child welfare directors, compact administrators and a large number of national child welfare organizations to provide recommendations for addressing the issues in the compact and its implementation. After intensive meetings and extensive communication with the states and outside stakeholders, APHSA disseminated two drafts of the rewritten compact—the Interstate Compact for the Placement of Children—for review and comment. The comments and concerns of the states and stakeholders have been compiled and integrated by APHSA staff and the Drafting Team. The third and final draft is forthcoming, with revisions completed by December 2005.

Organizations to Contact

The editors have compiled the following list of organizations concerned with the issues debated in this book. The descriptions are derived from materials provided by the organizations. All have publications or information available for interested readers. The list was compiled on the date of publication of the present volume; the information provided here may change. Be aware that many organizations take several weeks or longer to respond to inquiries, so allow as much time as possible.

Association of Administrators of the Interstate Compact on the Placement of Children
American Public Human Services Association
Washington, DC   20002
(202) 682-0100 • fax: (202) 289-6555
Web site: www.icpc.aphsa.org

The Association of Administrators of the Interstate Compact on the Placement of Children represents members from fifty states, the District of Columbia, and the U.S. Virgin Islands, who administer the Interstate Compact on the Placement of Children (ICPC). Its publications include *Guidebook to the ICPC* and *Understanding Delays in the Interstate Home Study Process.*

Bastard Nation
PO Box 1469, Edmond, OK   73083
(415) 704-3166
Web site: www.bastards.org

Bastard Nation is an advocacy group promoting the rights of adult citizens who were adopted as children. Its primary mission is the restoration of adoptees' rights to access their records. Its publications include *The Basic Bastard: The Bible of Adoptee Rights.*

Center for Adoption Policy (CAP)
168A Kirby Lane, Rye, NY   10580
Web site: www.adoptionpolicy.org

CAP is an organization with the goal of removing barriers to domestic and intercountry adoption. It provides research, analysis, and education to practitioners and the public about current adoption legislation and practices. Its publications include reports such as *Romanian Law—In the Best Interests of the Children?* and memoranda such as *Status of EU Member States' Ratification of International Conventions on Adoption Policies.*

Child Welfare League of America (CWLA)
2345 Crystal Dr., Suite 250, Arlington, VA   22202
(703) 412-2400 • fax: (703) 412-2401
Web site: www.cwla.org

The CWLA is the nation's oldest and largest membership-based child welfare organization. CWLA supports agencies that serve children and families through its research, education, and advocacy efforts. Its publications include the *Children's Voice* magazine, the *Child Welfare* journal, and the *Children's Monitor* online newsletter.

Coalition for Fair Adoption
PO Box 13184, St Petersburg, FL   33733
(813) 870-3735 • fax: (727) 490-0965
e-mail: fairadoption@eqfl.org
Web site: www.fairadoption.org

The Coalition for Fair Adoption is an organization committed to repealing Florida's ban on adoption and foster care by gays and lesbians. It educates the public about the effects of Florida's ban and advocates for a change in state policy. Among its publications are the monthly e-newsletter, *Equality Update* as well as *The High Cost of Permanency: An Analysis of the Economic Impact of Florida's Adoption Ban.*

Concerned Women for America
1015 Fifteenth St. NW, Suite 1100, Washington, DC   20005
(202) 488-7000 • fax: (202) 488-0806
Web site: www.cwfa.org

Concerned Women for America is an advocacy organization that promotes biblical values and a restoration of the American family to its traditional purpose. Its core issues are: family, the sanctity of human life, education, pornography, religious liberty, and national sovereignty. It publishes the bimonthly magazine, *Family Voice*.

Evan B. Donaldson Adoption Institute
120 E. 38th St., New York, NY   10016
(212) 925-4089 • fax: (775) 796-6592
e-mail: info@adoptioninstitute.org
Web site: www.adoptioninstitute.org

The Evan B. Donaldson Adoption Institute is a nonprofit organization dedicated to strengthening adoption policy and practice. The institute conducts research, educates the public, and promotes better policy and the translation of this policy into better adoption practice. Among its numerous publications are Adoption Attitudes National Surveys and various policy and practice papers, including *Adoption in the Schools: A Lot to Learn* and *Intercountry Adoption in Emergencies: The Tsunami Orphans*.

National Association of Black Social Workers (NABSW)
2305 Martin Luther King Ave. SE, Washington, DC   20020
(202) 678-4570 • fax: (202) 678-4572
Web site: www.nabsw.org

NABSW is committed to improving the quality of life and empowering people of African ancestry through advocacy, service, and research. The association takes positions on such issues as domestic violence, welfare reform, and kinship care. It publishes position papers and quarterly newsletters.

National Center for Adoption Law and Policy
303 E. Broad St., Columbus, OH   43215
(614) 236-6730 • fax:(614) 236-6958
e-mail: adoptionctr@law.capital.edu
Web site: www.law.capital.edu/adoption

The National Center for Adoption Law & Policy is an education, advocacy, and research organization based at the Capital
University Law School. The center's aim is to improve foster
care and adoption law, policies, and practices. It publishes a
newsletter, *Maestro Notes*, as well as weekly news summaries
and weekly case summaries.

National Council for Adoption (NCFA)
225 N. Washington St., Alexandria, VA   22314-2561
(703) 299-6633 • fax: (703) 299-6004
e-mail: ncfa@adoptioncouncil.org
Web site: www.adoptioncouncil.org

The council advocates for the positive option of adoption
while promoting the well-being of children, birth parents, and
adoptive families. NCFA is a research, education, and advocacy organization. It publishes the *Adoption Factbook*, the *National Adoption Report*, a monthly electronic newsletter, and
the *Adoption Advocate* magazine.

National Family Justice Association (NFJA)
PO Box 35, Hubbard, OH   44425
(330) 534-3510
e-mail: nfjainfo@aol.com
Web site: www.nfja.org

The NFJA's goal is to provide information about laws and
policies that are negatively affecting American families. NFJA
advocates reform in such areas as parental abduction, unjust
adoptions, and fraudulent paternity establishments. It publishes position statements and articles on these and other issues.

National Foster Care Coalition (NFCC)
1776 I St. NW, 9th Fl., Washington, DC   20006
(202) 756-4842
Web site: www.nationalfostercare.org

The coalition aims to improve the lives of children, youth, and adults in and from foster care. NFCC advocates on behalf of children and families involved in foster care, supports foster care initiatives, and offers training and education about foster care to policy makers.

North American Council on Adoptable Children (NACAC)
970 Raymond Ave., Suite 906, St. Paul, MN   55114
(651) 644-3036 • fax: (651) 644-9848
e-mail: info@nacac.org
Web site: www.nacac.org

The NACAC is an organization dedicated to waiting children and the families who adopt them. It promotes and supports permanent placement of children and youth in the United States and Canada, especially those in foster care and with special needs. NACAC publishes the quarterly newsletter *Adoptalk* as well as other publications such as *Achieving Permanence for Every Child: A Guide for Limiting the Use of Long-Term Foster Care as Its Permanent Plan* and *Barriers to Same Race Placement*.

Pew Commission on Children in Foster Care
e-mail: hcooper@pewtrusts.org
Web site: www.pewfostercare.org

The Pew Commission on Children in Foster Care is committed to finding ways to improve outcomes for children in the foster care system. In particular, it seeks to facilitate faster movement of children from foster care into safe, permanent homes and to improve court oversight of child welfare cases. It publishes reports such as *Fostering the Future: Safety, Permanence and Well-Being for Children in Foster Care* and *Demographics of Children in Foster Care*, as well as research reports and a newsletter.

Bibliography

Books

Naomi R. Cahn and Joan Heifetz Hollinger, eds.	*Families by Law: An Adoption Reader,* New York: New York University Press, 2004.
E. Wayne Carp	*Adoption Politics: Bastard Nation and Ballot Initiative 58,* Lawrence: University Press of Kansas, 2004.
Sara Dorow	*Transnational Adoption: A Cultural Economy of Race, Gender, and Kinship,* New York: New York University Press, 2006.
Sally Haslanger and Charlotte Witt, Eds.	*Adoption Matters: Philosophical and Feminist Essays,* Ithaca, NY: Cornell University Press, 2005.
Timothy P. Jackson, Ed.	*The Morality of Adoption: Social-Psychological, Theological, and Legal Perspectives,* Grand Rapids, MI: Wm. B. Eerdmans, 2005.
Barbara Melosh	*Strangers and Kin: The American Way of Adoption,* Cambridge, MA: Harvard University Press, 2006.
Kerry O'Halloran	*The Politics of Adoption: International Perspectives on Law, Policy & Practice,* New York: Springer, 2006.
Pamela Anne Quiroz	*Adoption in a Colorblind Society,* Lanham, MD: Rowman & Littlefield, 2007.

Barbara Katz Rothman	*Weaving a Family: Untangling Race and Adoption*, Boston: Beacon, 2006.
Lita Linzer Schwartz	*When Adoptions Go Wrong: Psychological and Legal Issues of Adoption Disruption*, Binghamton, NY: Haworth, 2006.
Lita Linzer Schwartz and Florence W. Kaslow, Eds.	*Welcome Home! An International and Nontraditional Adoption Reader*, Binghamton, NY: Haworth, 2004.
Jane Jeong Trenka, Julia Chinyere Oparah, Sun Yung Shin, Eds.	*Outsiders Within: Writing on Transracial Adoption*, Cambridge, MA: South End, 2006.
Toby Alice Volkman, ed.	*Cultures of Transnational Adoption*, Durham, NC: Duke University Press, 2005.
Katarina Wegar, ed.	*Adoptive Families in a Diverse Society*, New Brunswick, NJ: Rutgers University Press, 2006.

Articles

Carol Barbieri	"Your Mother Would Know," *New York Times*, November 29, 2005.
Vivian Berger	"Ban Hurts Children," *The National Law Journal*, April 4, 2005.
Daniel Bergner	"The Case of Marie and Her Sons," *New York Times Magazine*, July 23, 2006, p. 28.

Jennifer Chrisler "Bill Restricting Adoptions Deserves to Die," *Arizona Daily Star*, March 27, 2005, B4.

"Black Adoption: Are We Taking Care of Our Own?" *New York Beacon*, Jun. 29–July 5, 2005.

"Two Mommies or Two Daddies Will Do Fine, Thanks," *Time*, December 14, 2006.

Lynette Clemetson "Adoptions from Guatemala Face an Uncertain Future," *New York Times*, May 16, 2007, p. A12.

Lynette Clemetson "Working on Overhaul, Russia Halts Adoption Applications," *New York Times*, April 12, 2007, p. A10.

Lynette Clemetson and Ron Nixon "Breaking Through Adoption's Racial Barriers," *New York Times*, August 17, 2006, p. A1.

Brian Connelly "The Problem Behind Chinese Adoption," *The American Enterprise*, January/February 2004, p. 42.

James C. Dobson "Two Mommies Is One Too Many," *Time*, December 12, 2006.

Lorraine Dusky "Help Adult Adoptees Find Birth Parents," *USA Today*, May 12, 2003.

Jane Erikson "Single Mothers See No Need for Adoption Bill," *Arizona Daily Star*, March 23, 2006.

Geoffrey A. Fowler and Elizabeth Bernstein	"China Weighs Rules Restricting Adoptions," *Wall Street Journal*, December 20, 2006, p. D1.
Christina Frank	"International Adoption," *Working Mother*, May 2007, 61.
Steve Friess	"U.S. Government Scrutinizes Guatemalan Adoptions," *USA Today*, March 19, 2007, p. D6.
Jane Gross	"U.S. Joins Overseas Adoption Overhaul Plan," *New York Times*, December 11, 2007, p. A29.
Anita Hamilton	"When Foster Teens Find a Home," *Time*, June 5, 2006, 58.
Albert R. Hunt	"Slow But Steady Progress on Adoption," *Wall Street Journal*, August 28, 2002, p. A13.
Jeff Jacoby	"When Love Matters More than Blood," *Boston Globe*, January 2, 2005.
Vanessa James	"Outsourcing Family Ties," *Savoy*, June-July 2005, p. 34.
Mary Kay Kisthardt and Barbara Handschu	"Unwed Fathers," *The National Law Journal*, March 19, 2007.
Wendy Koch	"Number of Single Men Adopting Foster Kids Doubles," *USA Today*, June 15, 2007, p. A5.

Wendy Koch   "Russia Curtails American Adoptions," *USA Today*, April 11, 2007, p. A1.

Fred Kuhr   "Hope for Foster Kids," *The Advocate*, July 18, 2006, p. 36.

Marc Lacey   "Guatemala System Is Scrutinized as Americans Rush In to Adopt," *New York Times*, November 5, 2006.

Jeninne Lee-St. John   "A Mother's Choice," *Time*, September 25, 2006, p. 64.

Tamar Lewin   "Unwed Fathers Fight for Babies Placed for Adoption by Mothers," *New York Times*, March 19, 2006, p. A1.

Lawrence B. Lindsey   "The U.N. vs. Adoption," *Weekly Standard*, April 28, 2003, 22.

Calum MacLeod   "Chinese Shed Quiet Stigma of Adoption," *USA Today*, November 21, 2007, p. A13.

Kent Markus   "Why the System Failed Evan Scott," *Florida Times-Union*, January 29, 2005.

Jo McGowan   "To Welcome a Child: Gay Couples & Adoption," *Commonweal*, May 5, 2006, p. 8.

E.J. Montini   "Throwing Out Baby with Bath Water, On Purpose this Time," *Arizona Republic*, March 28, 2006.

Andy Newman and Rebecca Cathcart	"In an Adoption Hub, China's New Rules Stir Dismay," *New York Times*, December 24, 2006.
Clarence Page	"Why Deny Children Loving Homes?" *Philadelphia Tribune*, November 3, 2006, p. 7A.
Kit R. Roane	"Pitfalls for Parents: International Adoption Has Become Big Business, but Regulation Still Lags," *U.S. News & World Report*, June 6, 2005, p. 56.
Stephanie Robichaux	"Supporting Tribal Reconnections," *Children's Voice*, May-June 2007, p. 9.
Julian Sanchez	"All Happy Families," *Reason*, August-September 2005.
Katie Santich	"Photo Portraits Help Kids Get Adopted," *Orlando Sentinel*, November 12, 2007.
Craig S. Smith	"Romania's Orphans Face Widespread Abuse, Group Says," *New York Times*, May 10, 2006, p. A3.
Debra Spur	"Online Images Open a Heart, then a Home," *New York Times*, December 18, 2005.
Andrea Stone	"Both Sides Say Their Concern Is the Children," *USA Today*, February 21, 2006, p. A8.

Jacob Sullum	"Suffer the Children," *New York Times*, August 27, 2006.
	"Thank Deng Xiaoping for Little Girls," *Reason*, December 2007.
Deborah Sussman Susser	"Proposed Adoption Bill Impedes Single Parents," *Jewish News of Greater Phoenix*, March 31, 2006, p. 1.
Cal Thomas and Bob Beckel	"Adoption Politics: What's Best for the Kids?" *USA Today*, March 9, 2006, p. A21.
Pat Wingert	"When Adoption Goes Wrong," *Newsweek*, December 17, 2007, p. 58.
Jim Yardley	"China Tightens Adoption Rules, U.S. Agencies Say," *New York Times*, December 19, 2006.
Cathy Young	"Adoption Swindle Shafts Dads," *Reason Online*, March 28, 2006.
Cathy Young	"Stigmatizing Fathers," *Boston Globe*, January 24, 2005.

Index